Lenny and Jake Adventures

Lenny prodded the bag gently with his magic baton and the bird flew away. Then, slowly and carefully, Lenny moved in and drew back the zip.

The bag was full of money! There must have been a fortune, stuffed to its brim in one-pound and five-pound notes.

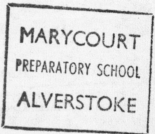

Also in Red Fox (incorporating Beaver Books) by Hazel Townson:

The Speckled Panic
The Choking Peril
The Barley Sugar Ghosts
Danny – Don't Jump
Pilkie's Progress
Gary Who?
The Moving Statue
Victor's Party

THE LENNY AND JAKE ADVENTURES
The Staggering Snowman
Fireworks Galore
Walnut Whirl

RED FOX READ ALONE BOOK
Through the Witch's Window
by Hazel Townson. Illustrated by Tony Ross

Hazel Townson
Lenny and Jake Adventures

Illustrated by Philippe Dupasquier

RED FOX

A Red Fox Book
Published by Random Century Children's Books
20 Vauxhall Bridge Road, London SW1V 2SA
A division of the Random Century Group

London Melbourne Sydney Auckland
Johannesburg and agencies throughout the world

The Great Ice-Cream Crime
First published by Andersen Press 1981; Beaver edition 1983
Text © Hazel Townson 1981
Illustrations © Andersen Press 1981

The Siege of Cobb Street School
First published by Andersen Press 1983; Beaver edition 1985
Text © Hazel Townson 1983
Illustrations © Andersen Press Ltd 1983

The Vanishing Gran
First published by Andersen Press Ltd 1983; Beaver edition 1985
Text © Hazel Townson 1983
Illustrations © Andersen Press Ltd 1983

Haunted Ivy
First published by Andersen Press Ltd 1984; Beaver edition 1986
Text © Hazel Townson 1984
Illustrations © Andersen Press Ltd 1984

Red Fox edition 1991

Printed and bound in Great Britain by
Cox & Wyman Ltd, Reading, Berkshire

ISBN 0 09 991800 5

1. The Great Ice-Cream Crime

Contents

1. The Dark Blue Shopping-bag   9
2. The Five-star Aunt   17
3. The Shock in the Cellar   37
4. The Church Jumble Sale   49
5. The Sponsored Hide-and-Seek   52
6. The Coal-black Apparition   58
7. The Five-star Princess   68

In memory of my sister-in-law, Cora Shaw,
and for Samantha

1
The Dark Blue Shopping-bag

It was the day the Princess was coming to open the new hospital, and all the schools had been given the morning off to line the route and cheer.

Lenny Hargreaves didn't intend to cheer. He had more important things than royalty to think of. He was going off into the woods by himself to practise his conjuring tricks. One day Lenny intended to be the star performer in

Magic Circle on television.

Lenny knew that the secret of being a good illusionist was secrecy, so he had taken to practising in the woods, where nobody but the birds could see.

Lenny's best friend, Jake Allen, was not magic-minded. He could have joined the act as Lenny's assistant, but had no wish to make a fool of himself. Maybe one day Lenny would really master the Disappearing Jampot and the Floating Aces tricks. In the meantime, Jake would stick to more down-to-earth amusements, such as stamp-collecting, or trying to spot all the Princess's private detectives.

It was a beautiful summer's day. All the children of Cobb Street Primary School – (except, of course, Lenny Hargreaves and a girl called Erica Carr who had chicken-pox) – marched in a crocodile to Redcross Road, which was where the new hospital stood. The hospital was on a hill, and its front windows had a pleasant view across fields and woods.

The Cobb Street children had been led to a strip of pavement just opposite the hospital's

main gates, and now, with their backs to the fields and woods, they packed themselves excitedly into the space right next to their old rivals, St. Bernard's Juniors, whom they jostled, booed and taunted. That was fun for a while, but then everyone began to grow hot, thirsty, bored and restless. To make things worse, they could see the ice-cream van in the field behind them, but were not allowed to run off and buy refreshments. The morning threatened to stretch out very long indeed, especially as the Princess was reported to be late. Jake Allen began to wish he had gone off to the woods with Lenny Hargreaves after all, and looked around desperately for a chance of escape.

Meanwhile, Lenny had found his usual spot at the foot of a beech tree in the middle of the woods. There he set up his lightweight, black-draped, folding table, ate half a bar of chocolate, and began:

'Ladies and gentlemen, today you will be privileged to see the Tenfold Trick, or how to finish up with ten times more money than you

started with. Here, you will observe, I have a ha'penny. I place it on the table, so, and cover it with this cloth. Now I pass my magic baton over it and say the magic words, "Zin, Zan, Zen, multiply by ten!"'

Lenny whipped away the cloth to reveal two coins instead of one – a ha'penny and a fivepenny piece. The ha'penny ought to have disappeared. Ignoring this slight hitch, Lenny continued:

'Now we cover up the fivepenny piece with the cloth and try again. Zin, Zan, Zen, multiply by ten!'

Once more Lenny whipped away the cloth to reveal a fifty-penny piece, only this time he whipped the cloth away so smartly that the fifty-penny piece flew through the air and almost disappeared from sight. Lenny ran after it. It lay in the grass beside a bit of paper which, to Lenny's utter astonishment, turned out to be a five-pound note! Lenny slapped his magic baton down on top of the fiver to stop it from blowing away, and that was when he spotted the dark blue mound half-hidden among the bracken under a nearby tree.

The dark blue mound looked like a shopping-bag, but surely a bulging shopping-bag was a curious thing to find lying among the bracken in a wood? Lenny eyed the bag warily. Perhaps it was a bomb.

Suddenly, a bird, chirruping noisily, alighted on the bag and hopped all the way along the zip to peck at one of the handles.

'Can't be a bomb, then,' Lenny thought, with a certain amount of disappointment, 'or the bird would have set it off.'

Lenny prodded the bag gently with his magic baton and the bird flew away. Then, slowly and carefully, Lenny moved in and drew back the zip.

The bag was full of money! There must have been a fortune, stuffed to its brim in one-pound and five-pound notes.

Speechlessly, Lenny gazed at his magic baton, then at the bag. At last he selected one of the notes and held it up to the light. There was that metal strip you were supposed to look for, to prove that the money was real. Lenny plunged his hands into the bag, just for the thrill of feeling all that money. What a staggering thing to happen! Could it have anything to do with his magic?

'Zin, Zan, Zen!' he whispered, thinking wildly of all the things that money could buy, from a solid gold bicycle to your own private island stacked with non-melting chocolate bars. But instead of the bag turning into ten bags of money, a shadow loomed behind Lenny, a hand fell heavily on to his shoulder and a voice cried, 'Caught you!'

2
The Five-star Aunt

Lenny Hargreaves lost his balance as he swung round to face his friend, Jake Allen.

'Idiot! You nearly frightened me to death! If you creep up on me like that again I'll have your brains for bike-oil.'

Jake stared at the bag of money.

'Hey, that's good! Is it your Zin-Zan-Whatsit trick?'

'It's not a trick – it's real money. I found it.'

Jake grinned. 'You're not the only one who plays Monopoly, you know.'

'I tell you it's *real money*.'

Jake took a closer look and was finally convinced. He was just as astounded as Lenny had been.

'What did you do, rob a bank?'

Lenny explained what had happened.

'Well, it certainly wasn't your magic. Somebody must have lost it. We'd better take it to the police.'

'Yes, I suppose so,' sighed Lenny, the vision of his chocolate island melting fast.

'There might be a reward,' Jake added hopefully. 'Here, give me one handle and I'll help you carry it.'

In a state of great excitement the two boys set off through the woods with the bag, speculating as to how the money could have been lost.

'Somebody sat down for a rest and left it behind.'

'Must have lost his memory, then.'

'It might have tumbled off the back of a horse.'

'Or fallen out of an aeroplane.'

'No, a helicopter.'

'Or somebody buried it and the rain washed the earth away. Or what if they buried it with a body, and then . . . .'

Their ideas grew wilder and wilder.

They must have walked at least a mile before Lenny suddenly stopped and groaned: 'My magic stuff! I've left it behind!'

Jake sneered disgustedly, but he knew they would have to go back. That equipment meant so much to Lenny. They plodded back in silence, but when they arrived at Lenny's beech tree there was no sign of the folding table and the box of tricks. Lenny couldn't believe it. He rushed around, kicking the bracken aside and scratching himself on the brambles.

'You sure you've got the right tree?'

''Course I'm sure! I've been practising here for weeks. Look, the ground's so soft just here that you can see my footprints anyway.'

Jake studied the ground.

'You've got one foot bigger than the other. Or else there's somebody else's footprints mixed in with yours.'

'You're right! Somebody's been here since we left and pinched my stuff. A big bloke, by the look of it.'

'Maybe you pinched his bag of money.'

'Well, he's not going to get away with my magic stuff. He can't have gone far. Let's see if we can catch him up. There's another big footprint. And one over there.'

The boys began to work their way through the wood once more, but this time in the opposite direction. Instead of coming out at the

golf-course end, they would now emerge in the fields across from the new hospital.

'We'll have to be careful no teacher spots us,' warned Jake, remembering the difficulties of slipping away earlier.

'I've lost track of the footprints now,' said Lenny.

Suddenly he stopped. 'Here, I wonder if all this money has anything to do with the Princess's visit?'

'How do you mean?'

'Well, just suppose you wanted somebody to

kidnap the Princess, or shoot her, or something. You'd have to pay them a lot of money.'

'You've been watching too much television,' sneered Jake.

'No, I haven't. In 1974 somebody tried to kidnap Princess Anne and her husband right in the middle of London, so there! Her chauffeur and her private detective got shot, and this man in a taxi who was following behind.' This item of news had made a great sensation at the time, and in fact Lenny's mother had kept the newspaper which had a picture of the shattered royal car.

Jake remembered that this was true. Lenny had even shown him the newspaper once. So now the thought crept into Jake's mind that perhaps Lenny was right. After all, it *was* a lot of money.

Jake sprang into life. 'Come on, then! The sooner we get to the police with this bag, the better.'

The boys began to run out of the woods and across the field towards Redcross Road, not caring any more whether teachers should see

them or not. In fact, all the better if they did. But of course when you want to be spotted, then nobody sees you at all.

The boys had passed no one in the woods, and the first sign of life they saw was Lucci's ice-cream van, parked at the far side of the field behind Redcross Road. The van had a queue, which a man and a woman in white coats were busy serving.

Jake was hot and thirsty. He would have loved an ice-cream, but knew there was no time to stop. They must grab the first policeman they saw – and there he was, standing right on the pavement edge in front of St. Bernard's Juniors.

Alas! Jake Allen was from the enemy camp. St. Bernard's Juniors wouldn't let him through.

'Get back, Allen!'

'Yeah, stick with your own rotten lot.'

'Give him a kick! Bloomin' cheek, barging in on our patch.'

Jake fought and struggled, but it was no use. He had about as much chance of reaching that policeman as he had of marrying the Princess. He even called out, but the policeman took no notice. Finally, bruised and battered, he withdrew.

Meanwhile, Lenny had spotted something. On the ground underneath Lucci's ice-cream van was a playing-card. Not an ordinary playing-card, but a trick one, with the top left-hand corner showing the four of hearts, and the bottom right-hand corner showing the nine of spades. It was exactly the same as one of the cards in Lenny's box of tricks.

'Hey!' cried Lenny angrily, leaping forward to grab the card.

He ran up to the ice-cream van with it and pushed his way to the front of the queue, meeting much the same opposition as Jake.

'There's a queue in case you hadn't noticed.'

'Get to the back and wait your turn.'

'Who does he think he is?'

But Lenny was oblivious of insult or injury.

'Have you got my magic stuff?' he called out to the ice-cream man. 'I want it back; it's mine!'

The white-coated couple both looked up at once. The man's eyes alighted on the dark blue shopping-bag which Lenny was still holding. A sudden, nasty change came over the man's face. He gave an unintelligible yell, then swung round to the back door of the van.

Sensing danger, Lenny fled. He heard the van door open and the ice-cream man shout again, but he didn't turn to look. Swiftly he caught up Jake and dragged him away round the back of the crowd towards the Cobb Street contingent.

'Quick! We've been spotted!'

Lenny plunged in among his cronies and Jake followed. Unlike St. Bernard's Juniors, the Cobb Street ranks obligingly gave way, and cheered their comrades on. Jake heard a bellow of rage behind him and turned to see a man in a white coat struggling after him. The look on that man's face made Jake feel cold all over.

Just as Jake thought the man was bound to reach out and grab him, a terrific cheer went up from the crowd. Two police motor-cyclists had appeared, riding sedately down the middle

of the road at the head of the Princess's motor-
cade. The great moment had come!

As the crowd surged forward, so Lenny and
Jake spilled forth onto the road. Seizing their
chance, they ran like mad to the other side, just
in time to avoid being mown down by the
motor-cyclists. The ice-cream man was not so
lucky. A policeman, leaping in to quell the
disturbance, grabbed him before he could dash
into the road, and kept him fuming helplessly
while the long, slow procession drove by,
slowing down even more to take the bend into

the hospital grounds.

The cheers were deafening; the excitement was intense. Even the weary teachers began to think the whole thing worth while as the Princess, in a gorgeous peacock-blue outfit, smiled and waved at them.

By the time the procession had passed into the hospital grounds, there was no sign of Jake and Lenny. They had run away down Orbit Street.

'Got to get rid of this bag,' panted Lenny. 'Hide it somewhere, then he daren't kill us till we've told him where it is.'

'*Kill* us?' echoed Jake in horror.

'One consolation, he won't do anything to the Princess either, until he gets his hands on the money. Where can we hide it quick?'

'How about my Aunt Ada's, just round the corner from here?'

Now it was Lenny's turn to follow, as Jake led the way to a neat little house at the end of a row.

'Won't your Aunt Ada be out watching the procession?'

'No, standing about too long makes her back ache. My dad says it runs in the family.'

Jake knocked on the door and a mumbly voice cried, 'Come in!' The two boys obeyed, closing the door thankfully after them.

'Hello, Aunt Ada. It's me and my friend Lenny Hargreaves. Just come to see how you are.'

Aunt Ada mumbled a greeting through a mouthful of pins, for she was dressmaking. She was a pleasant, plump lady with quick fingers and twinkly eyes, and nodded vigorous approval of the boys' visit. At least a three-star aunt, was Lenny's first impression.

'We're not stopping, Auntie. We just wondered if you'd do us a favour.'

'Hungry?' Aunt Ada's pin-stuck grin conveyed that she knew all about boys and the sort of favours they wanted.

'No, it's not that. We want you to look after something for us.'

Jake glanced at Lenny for help, and Lenny nodded encouragingly.

'It's a bag of money. Can we hide it some-

where?'

'Why not? Put it in the spare back bedroom if you like,' said Aunt Ada, stabbing home her last pin.

'We think it's worth about a million pounds. Do you want to look?'

'Not really, dear. I'll take your word for it. I'm trying to get finished before your Uncle Bert comes home for his lunch.'

Aunt Ada stuffed the edge of a pale blue garment under the foot of the sewing-machine and stepped on the starter-button. The machine began to hum, the cloth moved steadily backwards, and Aunt Ada's quick fingers began to pluck away the pins she had just put in so carefully. She was leaning forward, concentrating so hard that she did not even turn as the boys went off upstairs with the dark blue shopping-bag.

Jake looked carefully out of the bedroom window, to make sure the coast was clear. The ice-cream man must never know they had been here. Mind you, if he did find out, he'd have Uncle Bert to contend with, and Uncle Bert

had been a well-known local amateur wrestler in his younger days.

Jake had a good look around the bedroom and decided to hide the bag in the bottom of a wardrobe which contained a few old dresses Aunt Ada no longer wore. They were probably awaiting the next Church jumble sale. One of the dresses had fallen from its hanger, so Jake draped it over the shopping-bag as an extra precaution. Then he re-checked that the street was empty and the boys went downstairs.

34

'Thanks, Auntie. We'll have to be going now.'

'Don't you want some ginger parkin?' cried Aunt Ada in amazement. 'I've only just baked it. I'm surprised you didn't smell it as soon as you came in.'

What a pity, but there really was no time for refreshments. If the Princess was to be saved, the boys must move fast.

'Thanks all the same, Auntie, but we have to go. Don't tell anyone about the money, will you?'

'My lips are sealed,' replied Aunt Ada solemnly. 'Give my love to your mum and dad, then.'

The boys slipped out of the front door to the accompaniment of the hum of the sewing-machine, and Aunt Ada shouting, 'Whoops!' as her needle ran off the edge of the hem.

'Definitely a five-star aunt!' said Lenny.

3
The Shock in the Cellar

'Where to now?' asked Lenny.

'Police station, of course. Let them sort it out.'

The boys ran all the way, and when they arrived they found Constable Barlow sitting alone by the telephone, furtively filling in his football coupon. Everyone else was out on procession duty.

'There's going to be an assassination or

something,' Lenny blurted out.

'Somebody's after the Princess,' added Jake.

A wary look came into Constable Barlow's eye. He'd had trouble with young lads like this before.

'It's not April First, you know,' he told them sternly. 'And the police force isn't half as daft as you think it is.'

'It's the ice-cream man,' continued Lenny.

'Well, him and a woman, both strangers, though it still says "Lucci's Ices" on the van.'

'Now, you look here . . .' began Constable Barlow, but he couldn't get another word in. Lenny and Jake were both talking at once.

'I was doing my conjuring in the wood . . . .'

'His fifty pence flew away and landed on a fiver . . . .'

'And then I saw this dark blue shopping-bag with about a million pounds in it . . . .'

'And he hit it with his magic baton and then we found all these notes . . . .'

'And I thought it was a bomb but it wasn't . . . .'

'And they're real because they've all got

metal bits . . . .'

Constable Barlow brought his fist down on the top of the desk with a thump.

'Shut up, the pair of you! That's better! Now, listen to me. We're having a hard enough day as it is, without you kids starting. Do you know what it's like, having a royal visit right through the middle of your patch?'

The Constable went on to describe at length the agonies of such a task.

'But it's *true!*'

'Don't you believe us?'

'We wouldn't make up a story like that.'

'We're trying to help, and I'll bet you'd get promoted or knighted or something if you saved her life.'

Constable Barlow flapped his hands despairingly.

'All right, all right! Go on, then, give us a bit of proof. Let's see this bag of money for a start.'

'We haven't got it. The ice-cream man was chasing us, so we hid it.'

'Hid it where?'

'We can't tell you that. Suppose this room's

bugged . . . .'

'Yes, they might be listening in.'

'Oh, give me strength!' prayed Constable Barlow. 'If you two aren't off these premises in ten seconds flat, I'll bundle you into the cells, so help me!' He rushed furiously round the desk, put a hand on each boy's back and swept both lads to the door.

'Go on, get out of it!'

'I don't know why we bother,' grumbled Lenny. 'Nobody ever believes a thing we say.'

He and Jake slunk moodily round the corner – and immediately spotted the ice-cream man again. He was moving towards them, and saw them at once.

Luckily, the boys were near to a bus stop. Jake ran to flag down the bus that mercifully appeared, and they both jumped on to it.

'Phew! That was close!'

'What if he follows us in a taxi?'

'Well, at least we're drawing him away from the Princess. We're saving her life. How long is she staying at the hospital?'

'At least an hour. Apart from the opening

ceremony, she's going round all the wards, chatting to the patients to cheer them up.'

'Right, then we've time to ride as far as the Post Office. We'll go into a call-box and ring up Buckingham Palace.'

'We don't know the number,' Jake pointed out.

'We'll soon find out,' retorted Lenny confidently. He walked straight into the call-box and dialled Directory Enquiries.

'Please could you give me the number of Buckingham Palace?'

Lenny was quite unprepared for the fervour with which the operator told him to get off the line or else.

'And I know which phone box you're in, so you needn't think you can vandalise it, either!'

'Crusty old cow!' grumbled Lenny. 'It'll be her fault now if the Princess gets murdered.'

'We could send a telegram to the Queen.'

'I've only 5p left. How about you?'

'Sevenpence,' Jake concluded gloomily, having searched every one of his pockets.

'Anyway, I suppose a telegram would take too long.'

'We could go round to the factory and tell your dad,' said Lenny, whose own dad was a long-distance lorry-driver and not readily available. 'Your dad would know what to do.'

'Yeah, that's a good idea. The only thing is, he told me not to hang around the factory any more. My mum's scared I'll fall in the canal.'

'It's an emergency, in case you'd forgotten.'

'Oh, all right. Come on, then. We'll take the short cut across the Deads.'

The 'Deads' was the children's name for a block of empty houses which were waiting to be pulled down. The trouble was that the Council had run out of money, so nobody was actually working on the job. The houses sat there, dirty and silent, with their doors and windows boarded up and their roofs falling in. Some of the houses even had wooden props to hold them up.

'Gives me the shivers, coming round here,' admitted Jake. 'I'll bet there are rats.'

'Old tramps and squatters, more likely.'

'Squatters? You'd have to be pretty desperate to squat round here.'

'I once had a dream that I came down here
at night and there was this crippled old hag
hunched up in a corner in a long, black cloak,
and her face was all twisted sideways....'

'Hey, what's that noise?' Jake had stopped
and grabbed Lenny's arm.

Lenny listened. He heard the 'Teddy Bears'
Picnic' tune, being played by Lucci's ice-cream
van not too far away.

'Quick! Dash into the nearest house!'

'We can't. They're all boarded up.'

It was true. The boys ran along the row like
frightened mice in search of a hole, and all the
time the sound of the ice-cream van was drawing nearer. Only when they reached the last
house did Jake and Lenny see a ray of hope.
The boards across one of its glassless windows
had been disturbed.

'We could climb in there!' cried Jake at
once, and that was exactly what they did, the
back half of Lenny disappearing from sight just
as Lucci's ice-cream van turned the corner into

the street.

It was gloomy inside the house, the only light coming in from the broken boards of the downstairs window. Jake and Lenny stood still for a while, recovering their breath and letting their eyes grow accustomed to the dark.

'Tune's stopped!' whispered Jake.

'I'll bet they're right outside. They'll see where we came in.'

'Come on, then! We'd better go down the cellar.'

Worn stone steps at the back of the house led

down into an even darker place which smelled damp and nasty. The boys didn't fancy it much, but it was certainly better than being captured by assassins. There was a door at the top of the steps, and Lenny closed this after him, wondering whether they could find anything to barricade it with. Surely there would be some kind of rubbish in a cellar? Barrels, and stuff like that. He was about to suggest a search when Jake grabbed his arm once more.

'Hear that?' he asked in a croaky whisper. 'There's somebody – or something – over in that corner.'

4
The Church Jumble Sale

When Uncle Bert came home for his lunch, Aunt Ada told him of the boys' visit.

'They were playing some sort of a game,' she said. 'Bank robbers or something, you know what boys are. Always has plenty of imagination, has our Jake. Takes after his mother.'

Uncle Bert grunted, remembering the imaginative patterns on the ties and socks Jake's mother gave at Christmas. Then he sat down to his hot meal, grumbling at the crowds which had made him late home.

'Don't know why they need a Princess to open a hospital. It's only a matter of cutting a bit of ribbon. You could have done it yourself in ten seconds with your dressmaking shears.'

'Oh, I daresay you're right!' Aunt Ada knew better than to argue with her husband. It was always wiser to change the subject, so she said:

'Don't forget, on your way back to work this afternoon you promised to take those old clothes to the Church Hall for the jumble sale. I

promised Mrs Potts she could have them by two o'clock, to leave plenty of time to sort them out for tonight. There are some old shoes in a bag in the bottom of the wardrobe. Better take those, too.'

'Jumble sale!' muttered Uncle Bert disgustedly. 'You'll be wanting a Princess to open *that* next news!'

'Here, try a bit of parkin,' said Aunt Ada soothingly. She cut a very large piece indeed.

5
The Sponsored Hide-and-Seek

Suddenly, a lamp was switched on in a corner of the cellar, and a voice called: 'How did you know where I was?'

It was a girl's voice, and it sounded familiar.

'Who's that?' asked Jake, momentarily blinded by the bright light rising from somewhere near the floor.

'It's Erica Carr!' cried Lenny in amazement.

'It can't be! She's off school with chicken-pox.'

'It *is* me,' said Erica. 'I haven't got chicken-pox, and I'm glad you've come. It wasn't so bad till they left me on my own.'

Erica Carr was the girl who sat next to Lenny in class. Her dad was the richest dad ever to be seen at Cobb Street Primary School. He wore good suits all the time and had a real leather briefcase. Sometimes he brought Erica to school in his Jaguar car. It was certain that Erica would not be allowed to play in an empty house in the Deads all by herself.

'What are you doing here?' Lenny asked her.

'It was supposed to be a sponsored hide-and-seek, for charity. At least, that's what they said last night. You get so much an hour for as long as you stay hidden.'

The boys saw that Erica was installed in some comfort on a mattress, surrounded by pillows, blankets, comics, refreshments and a reading-lamp.

'I say! It's quite a set-up!' cried Jake admiringly, paying particular attention to a bottle of

lemonade and the remains of a custard pie.

'Yes, I thought it was fun at first,' agreed Erica ruefully. 'Especially when they said how much money we were going to make for the new hospital. And last night we had fish and chips for supper and played snakes-and-ladders, and they said I'd have my picture in the papers.'

'*Who* said?'

'This man and woman from Lucci's ice-cream van. They said Mr Lucci was playing as well, hiding somewhere on the other side of town. I just went to buy an ice-cream on my way home from school, and they told me all about it.'

'Erica, you chump! Don't you see, you're not in a sponsored hide-and-seek, you're a hostage? That couple from the ice-cream van are out to get the Princess, and they've captured you first so that if anything goes wrong they'll have something to bargain with.'

'I'm not a chump!' objected Erica. 'I guessed there was something wrong this morning when they said they were going to get the money.

You don't collect sponsor-money until it's all over, and I was still supposed to be hiding. They wouldn't have known how much to collect. I'd have gone home, only I fell down the cellar steps when we came in, and I've hurt my ankle. They bandaged it up for me, but I can't walk.'

'Poor old Erica! Never mind, we'll rescue you now, and you'll probably still get your picture in the papers for being a hostage.'

'What about *them?*' asked Jake. 'Don't forget they're chasing us, which is why we ran in here in the first place.'

Even as he spoke, there came a sound of splintering wood, followed by shouts and thuds. Then suddenly there was a terrific crash right over their heads. The foundations shook, there was a din like an exploding bomb, and a great cloud of dust rose up from nowhere, making the children choke and cough.

'What – what's happening?' There were more rumblings and tumblings.

'I think the house has fallen down.'

'Fallen on top of us? You mean we're

trapped in here?'

'Looks like it.' Jake had run up the cellar steps and found the doorway completely blocked. 'Mind you, somebody will have heard the din. They're sure to come and rescue us after a bit. You needn't be scared, Erica.'

'I'm not scared. I just wish it *was* a sponsored hide-and-seek. Think how much money we'd be making.'

'That's the stuff, Erica! Tell you what, when we get out of here you can be my conjuror's assistant if you like,' said Lenny generously.

6
The Coal-black Apparition

The police car, its siren wailing, pulled up with a screech in the middle of the Deads, and a couple of policemen leapt out to survey the damage.

'Collapsed like a house of cards,' said one.

'Well, Fred, we warned the Council, didn't we? We told 'em this lot wasn't safe.'

In the few minutes since the house had fallen, quite a crowd had gathered. It was amazing, thought Fred, where people suddenly appeared from in a crisis. Ten to one there hadn't been a soul in sight five minutes ago.

'Now then, stand back, please! Stand right back! This lot's dangerous!'

Fred turned to his companion. 'Get some more lads down here, George. We want a cordon across both ends of the street. Have to get rid of all these sightseers.'

'There's somebody under there,' a voice cried. 'We were trying to dig him out.'

'It's Mr Lucci,' a woman shouted. 'There's his van, all bashed about. He must have got out of it just when the shop started falling.'

'It's not Mr Lucci, it's a red-head. I saw him just before the wall went down.'

'All right, all right! Let's leave it to the experts. Fire engine's on its way.'

'He might be dead by the time that gets here. You want to do something now.'

'We'll get to him, missus, don't you worry. But if you start jumping about all over that lot you'll only make things worse.'

While all this activity was going on outside,

Jake had been mooching thoughtfully round the cellar.

'There's all black grit in this corner,' he said at last.

'That'll be coal-dust,' Lenny explained. He remembered that his grandma had lived in a house like this when she was young. She had often described it to him. All the houses had coal fires then, and the cellar was used to keep the coal in.

Suddenly Lenny had an idea. 'They didn't carry the coal in down all those steps. The coalman used to tip it through a little door at street level.'

Lenny looked up. Somewhere up there was another little door which might not be blocked with rubble.

'Can you see anything?'

'Put the light out for a minute.'

Jake switched off the light, and Lenny cried: 'There you are! Two little chinks of daylight!'

Lenny climbed up onto an old stone bench and borrowed Jake's knife. He worked the knife blade into one of the chinks of light and followed it round. He discovered a wooden flap with a metal catch on it, but the catch had rusted and he was able to force it outwards with the knife. Dirt and rust fell in onto Lenny's head, but he could smell fresh air.

'Give me a push!'

Jake climbed up beside Lenny on the bench, and hoisted him upwards. At last, Lenny managed to wriggle his head and shoulders into the gap. There was a lot of rubble out there, but he thought he could clear a way through it. He pulled out his arms and started moving the debris in front of him, stone by stone.

A second police car had just arrived on the scene, bringing two more senior officers. They took over immediately, issuing orders in all directions. Fred was actually on his way to carry out one of those orders at the double when he almost fell over a coal-black apparition which appeared on the ground in front of him. It was Lenny, torn and filthy but triumphant.

Lenny was amazed at the devastation that met his eyes, but he wasn't half as amazed as Fred who had nearly trodden on Lenny's face.

Needless to say, Lenny wasted no time in telling his story. There were two murderers under that rubble, foiled in the act of catching the Princess. There was also their hostage who thought she was on a sponsored hide-and-seek. Once more the tale of the dark blue shopping-bag started, but long before it was finished Fred had concluded that Lenny was suffering from shock.

'Better get him to hospital!'

'Poor lad, he isn't half in a state!'

'Come on, son,' the policeman said kindly,

removing his jacket and covering Lenny's shoulders with it. 'Let's get you down to the car.'

Lenny grew frantic with the desperation of wanting to be believed.

'Go and look in that ice-cream van,' he insisted. 'You'll find a conjuring set that belongs to me . . . .'

''Course we will,' Fred replied, humouring him. 'Now, just you get into that seat and relax. We'll have you down at the hospital in no time.'

And that was how Lenny Hargreaves finished up in the Casualty Department of the new hospital, being pushed along a corridor in a wheelchair, just as the Princess's visit was coming to an end.

The royal party was at one end of the corridor, about to turn away to the main entrance and depart, when the Princess spotted Lenny's wheelchair at the other end. The Princess stopped to enquire what had happened to Lenny. A nurse explained about the collapse of the building. Then, ignoring her

schedule, the Princess moved sympathetically towards the wheelchair. Lenny felt giddy with relief. At last he could seize a wonderful opportunity to deliver his warning face to face.

'Please, your Royal Highness, there's an ice-cream man out to get you. Somebody's paid him a fortune, and he's either going to kidnap you or shoot you or something . . . .'

Before the Princess had time to react, officials moved in swiftly, somebody gestured, the nurse turned Lenny's chair and moved away, and the Princess was spirited off along another corridor. It all happened so quickly that Lenny was no longer sure he had actually talked to the Princess. Maybe he was suffering from shock after all.

'We'll put you into a nice, warm bed, dear, and give you some medicine to calm you down,' the nurse said soothingly to Lenny.

'Oh, I give up!' groaned Lenny Hargreaves. 'You'll only believe me when it's too late.'

67

7
The Five-star Princess

The firemen dug carefully through the rubble.
They found a man and a woman, both wearing
ice-cream jackets, and both with broken legs.
They also found a couple of children in the
cellar, both of them black as the jack of spades.

So, a little while later, Erica Carr and Jake
Allen joined Lenny Hargreaves in the children's ward at the new hospital. Jake was put
into the bed next to Lenny, and immediately

asked him why they were being treated like dying soldiers.

'They think we're suffering from shock, having hallucinations or something.'

'Yeah,' Jake agreed gloomily. 'I told them about you finding that fiver, and then the bag of money, and they thought I'd dreamed it.'

'Grown-ups are stupid sometimes.'

'Wait till my parents get here,' called Erica from the bed across. 'Everyone will listen to us then.'

It was not long before Mr and Mrs Carr appeared, looking pale and wild. Mrs Carr flung her arms round Erica and burst into tears, while Mr Carr put *his* arms round both of them together, and patted them both on the shoulders. Lenny thought he saw a tear roll down Mr Carr's cheek as well, but he could have been mistaken.

After the touching family reunion, Jake and Lenny defied all nurses' protests and joined the group round Erica's bed. Then, bit by bit, the story was pieced together.

'They said you had the list of people sponsoring my hide-and-seek,' said Erica to her mother, 'so I thought you'd know where I was.'

'She was really a hostage, of course,' explained Lenny, 'but we rescued her.'

'Well, not a hostage exactly,' said Mr Carr.

'The kidnappers warned us not to tell the police about Erica,' Mrs Carr went on, 'so we rang up the school and said she had chicken-pox.'

'Kidnappers?' echoed Jake.

'Yes, I'm afraid that's what they were. I left the ransom money in the woods, as they told me to. Then I went back later, expecting Erica to be there in exchange, but of course she wasn't. That was a terrible moment,' Mr Carr remembered, 'because the money had gone, yet the kidnappers had not kept their word.'

'Just a minute!' yelled Lenny. 'Did you say *in the woods?* You left the ransom money in the woods? In a dark blue shopping-bag?'

'That's right. The kidnappers took the money. We'll never see that again, but as long as we have Erica safe and sound, that's all that matters.'

'No, they didn't take the money,' cried Lenny, seeing everything clearly at once. 'We took it! It's at the bottom of his Aunt Ada's wardrobe.'

Here he pointed to Jake, who said nobody need worry, the money was safe and sound, because he'd wrapped it up in his Aunt Ada's old brown frock.

'What about the Princess, then?'

'False alarm. We got a bit mixed up,' grinned Jake.

'You mean nobody was going to shoot her or anything? No wonder they thought we were barmy!'

At that moment the ward sister appeared.

'Come on, you two, back into bed! The doctor's coming to look at you.'

Meanwhile, back at the police station, Constable Barlow picked up the telephone for the umpteenth time and wished it had never been invented. But this time the caller was his wife.

'Is that you, Ben? Oh, thank goodness for that! I've just had the most terrible shock.'

'Look here, Jenny, you can't go ringing me

up at work. We've no end of a crisis on here, and I can't sit talking to you. Got to keep the line free for important calls.'

'*This* is an important call, Ben Barlow! I've just had the shock of my life, I tell you! There I was, sorting out jumble at the Church Hall, and what did I find? Only a shopping-bag stuffed full of money, that's all!'

So in the end Jake and Lenny were listened to after all, and their story even found its way

into the newspapers. Maybe that was where the Princess saw it. At any rate, she found out what had been going on, and not long afterwards the boys received a parcel with the royal crest on it. The contents included a brand new conjuring outfit and the biggest packet of foreign stamps you ever saw.

'Definitely a five-star Princess,' Lenny said.

2. The Siege of Cobb Street School

For my lovely new family—
My son's wife Christine and
My daughter's husband David.

1

It was the last day of term. Only Miss Pritchard's class was in school, because all the others were out on their end-of-term excursions. Miss Pritchard's class had had its excursion yesterday, to collect its prize in the Young Observer Collage Competition. The magnificent winning collage, mounted on thick board, now hung proudly on the classroom wall.

After yesterday's excitement there was an air

of anti-climax. School seemed half-dead without the other classes—just when a spot of boasting could have been quite enjoyable, too. No morning assembly; no proper lessons; just a long, boring wait until noon, when the main summer holiday would begin.

Miss Pritchard was reading a story. After that it would be playtime. Then a quick general knowledge quiz, and the great rush to freedom.

Lenny Hargreaves stifled a yawn. He had already watched a version of this story on television and knew how it would end. Trust old Pritty to pick one like that! Lenny began to daydream about his latest magic trick. The Flying Paperclips, it was called. You threw a handful of loose paperclips into the air and let them fall into an empty paper bag. You shook the bag, said the magic words, and hey presto!—you drew out the paperclips all fastened together in a long line. Really spectacular! He was going to use it as his opening trick at his forthcoming Charity Show in his dad's garage.

Lenny was rudely awakened by a kick on the ankle from his friend, Jake Allen, who sat right behind him. He turned to scowl at Jake, who gave him a slow and solemn wink. Then Jake's hand shot up.

Miss Pritchard sighed. 'Yes, Jake, what is it?'

'Please may I fetch Lenny a glass of water, Miss? He's not feeling too good.'

Lenny began a startled shout of protest, but it came out more like a croak. Miss Pritchard, fearing the worst, sent Lenny out at once to get a drink and a breath of fresh air, and asked Jake to look after him.

'How about that? Worked a treat!' Jake shouted gleefully when they were out of earshot.

'Rotter! Suppose I'd been listening to the story?'

'Well, you weren't. I could almost hear you snoring. Anyway, it's been on telly. Everybody knows how it ends.'

'Liar, then, saying I was ill when I'm not.'

'I didn't say you were ill. I said you weren't feeling too good, meaning angelic. When did you last feel angelic, Lenny Hargreaves?'

'All right, Clever Clogs, what do we do now?'

'Come on, we'll sit on the pipes in the cloakroom. I've got some crisps in my anorak pocket.'

It was from the cloakroom window that Jake spotted the two men crossing the school playground in a hurry. They were dressed in boiler-suits and carried plumbers' bags.

'If you want a drink you'd better be quick. It looks as though the plumbers have come to

turn the water off.'

'You'd think they could have waited until we'd all gone home.'

'My mum say workmen do it on purpose.'

'Do what?'

'Make everything as inconvenient as possible. She says it gives them a kick.'

'Yeah, like bus drivers who see you coming and won't wait.'

'They've gone down to the boiler-house,' reported Jake, still at the window.

'Huh! Why couldn't the boiler go out of action in the middle of the winter term, so we'd all get sent home! Just our luck!'

'Never mind, have some crisps.'

The two boys sat munching contentedly, never dreaming of the crisis that was about to transform their lives. For how could Jake and Lenny have guessed that the two 'plumbers' were already taking out guns from their plumbers' bags? Or that in a couple of minutes' time those two men would be creeping carefully along by the wall towards the door of Miss Pritchard's room?

2

Miss Pritchard's story was drawing to a close. Her voice had slowed down because she was trying to keep everyone guessing. Suspense, that was the important ingredient of story-telling. She noted with satisfaction that her method worked, too. Some of the class had been fidgeting quite brazenly all through the story, but were now sitting perfectly still, eyes wide, ears strained. She smiled, allowing a short, dramatic pause.

It was then that Miss Pritchard became aware of the draught from the door behind her. She was aware of a presence, too. Someone had opened that door, and now stood at her back. In fact, it was this someone who had caused the class to pay so much attention. They were not listening to the story at all.

Miss Pritchard turned . . . to see a man in a boiler-suit, pointing a long-barrelled gun at the class. The man advanced into the room, revealing a second man behind him. The second man's gun was aimed right at Miss Pritchard's head.

Miss Pritchard stared, feeling just as confused and speechless as the class.

'All right,' said the first man, whose name was Stone. 'Do as you are told, and nobody will get hurt. We just want you to sit nice and still for half an hour or so, while we make a couple of telephone calls. After that, with a bit of luck, you can all go home as usual.'

Miss Pritchard took a deep breath.

'I don't know who you think you are, but this is no sort of joke to play on young children. If

this is some students' rag . . . .'

The second gunman, whose name was Dagget, moved forward.

'Save your breath, love,' he said quite kindly. 'It won't make any difference.'

Miss Pritchard had no intention of saving her breath.

'Put that gun away at once! And stop frightening these children. Are you completely irresponsible?'

'No, as a matter of fact, we're not,' Stone replied patiently. 'We're here for a very responsible purpose. I've told you, nobody will be hurt if you do as we say. All we want is to save a friend of ours from serving a long prison sentence for something he didn't do. That's not irresponsible, is it?' He appealed to the class. 'You'd stick up for *your* friends if they were in trouble, wouldn't you?'

'Course they would!' Dagget answered for the petrified children.

'I see!' said Miss Pritchard grimly. 'You think you can use us as hostages to help you get your own way, is that it?'

'Full marks!' Stone smiled at the class. 'She's clever, your teacher.'

Miss Pritchard looked positively thunderous.

'I call that irresponsible, and a lot besides. Anyway, if you must have a hostage, you can have me. These children are all expected home at just after twelve, and if they don't turn up . . . .'

'Exactly!' Stone smiled again, like a man-eating tiger looking forward to its dinner. 'Cause quite a panic, wouldn't it?'

'You mean you are going to keep all these children here indefinitely?' Two pink spots began to burn angrily in Miss Pritchard's cheeks. 'Well, of course, you'll never get away with it.'

'Oh, I don't know! It's surprising what people get away with these days. Hi-jackings, bank robberies, assassinations; sieges and sit-ins and snipings. Besides, we're not asking for much. Just the release of our friend, a helicopter to get him away, and enough money for our escape. We're not greedy. It shouldn't take long to arrange, either, once we start the telephoning. Now, why don't you just relax? Take it easy, do as we say, and we'll all come out of it smiling!'

As he said this, Stone began to retreat towards the doorway.

'All right,' he told Dagget, 'I'll go and make those calls now. Any trouble and you know what to do.'

Dagget nodded, closing the door after Stone and stationing himself in front of it.

'Right!' he smiled round at the class. 'No

reason why you shouldn't get on with your lessons while you're waiting. It'll help to pass the time.'

Miss Pritchard scowled at the clock. 'It happens to be playtime.'

'All right, play, then. At your desks, of course. No moving about.'

'These children need to move about. They've been sitting still since half-past nine. They need exercise and fresh air and . . . .'

Dagget suddenly turned nasty.

'Look, lady, I've heard enough from you. Either you do as you're told, or somebody's going to get hurt. Is that clear?'

Somewhere at the back of the room a child began to whimper.

3

Lenny Hargreaves looked at his watch.

'It's five minutes into playtime. Where is everybody?'

'Looks like that story's still dragging on.'

'More likely everybody's fallen asleep.'

'Shall we go back and wake them up?'

'Not likely! I'm having my full quarter of an hour.'

The crisps were all eaten, so they started on a ball of chewing-gum which Lenny had found in a corner of his hanky. The chewing-gum was tasteless. What's more, playtime came and went with still no sign of the class.

'Do you suppose Pritty's let everybody go home early?'

'No chance! Still, something must be up. Let's go and peer through the windows.'

'It's a miracle she's not sent somebody to look for us by now. We could both be lying dead.'

'Forgotten all about us, I shouldn't wonder.' Lenny sounded hurt.

The two boys crept along by the wall, much as the gunmen had done, until they reached the outside of Miss Pritchard's classroom. Cobb Street Junior School was old, and the dark stone windowsills were high. There were, however, certain well-known footholds underneath, which Jake stepped neatly into.

Five seconds later he was dragging Lenny excitedly back towards the cloakroom.

'It's a hold-up! There's this bloke with a gun. Lucky he didn't see me. I think it's one of those plumbers.'

'Ha ha! Very funny!' sneered Lenny.

'No, honestly!' Jake described in detail the scene he had just glimpsed through the classroom window. He was so upset that Lenny reluctantly began to believe him. After all, the rest of the class still hadn't appeared.

'Let me have a look!'

'Don't be daft, he might see you!'

'Well, we can't just hang about. We've got to *do* something.'

'Raise the alarm.'

'Ring the police, you mean? They'll never

believe us. Remember what happened that time we found the bag of money?'

'They won't know who we are. We'll go to the office and dial 999. If we ask for fire, police and ambulance something's bound to turn up. They won't dare ignore us in case it really is an emergency.'

'I wouldn't bet on it. They'll be able to tell how old we are. Police never believe anyone under twenty-one. Pity Mrs Gladstone's away on the school trip. She could have done it.' Mrs Gladstone was the school secretary.

By now they were nearing the office, but Jake suddenly pulled up. He could see, through the half-open office door, a gunman standing there with the telephone in his hand. Luckily, the gunman had his back to the door.

'Oh, come on now,' Stone was saying, 'that's not much of a price to pay for a teacher and twenty-eight kids.'

Jake felt weak with horror as he realised what was happening. Suspicions were all very well, but now they knew for sure. They'd have to think fast. He shooed Lenny silently into the

room opposite the office, which happened to be the staff-room.

'Out of sight, quick!'

At the back of the staff-room was an ancient wardrobe, which seemed to be the handiest place to hide.

'Did you hear what he said?' whispered Jake from behind Miss Pritchard's voluminous macintosh.

'Yes. Holding us to ransom, then.'

'It's a siege!'

'And to think we wouldn't have been here at all today if we hadn't won a prize with our rotten collage.'

After a long, gloomy silence, Lenny said: 'It's all up to us, then, isn't it? We've got the only advantage. Those gunmen don't know we're here. Twenty-eight kids, I heard him say. But there are thirty of us. Maybe we can take them by surprise.'

'Us and who else?' Jake muttered glumly.

4

Miss Pritchard was not an easy enemy. Nearing retirement after a lifetime of teaching, she was wise in the ways of errant youngsters, and particularly bullies. The gunmen might think themselves grown-up, but to Miss Pritchard they were still youngsters misbehaving in a childish and particularly unacceptable fashion. If they thought they could scare her, they were very much mistaken.

Miss Pritchard was a bulky woman, with

two chins and a lot of tightly-permed grey hair. Her nickname, like most people's, was the opposite of the truth. She was not, and never had been, pretty, but there are other qualities more valuable than good looks in a crisis.

'All right, children,' said Miss Pritchard briskly, 'we'll carry on with the general knowledge quiz. Divide yourselves up into the usual four teams, A B C and D. I'll keep the score on the blackboard. Fiona, for goodness' sake stop snivelling. You don't know when you're lucky, my girl. Think of the tale you'll have to tell when you get home today. You'll be the centre of attention.'

Fiona stopped snivelling and wiped her eyes on her cardigan sleeve.

'Right, Barry, we'll begin with you. What is the capital city of Sweden?'

'Er—Stockholm, Miss.'

'Right! One point for team A.' Miss Pritchard marked up the score. 'Now, Jane. Which is the longest river in the world?'

The quiz picked up speed and the children became interested. Some of them were so

proud of their correct answers that they even stole sideways glances at the gunman to see if he appreciated their cleverness.

But Dagget had other things on his mind. He wished Stone would hurry up with the telephoning. He wished he could already hear that helicopter landing on the playing field behind the school. He wished the whole thing was over, and they were all safe in their hideout in the south of France.

Dagget was restless. He shifted his feet. Then he took a few paces away from the door towards

Miss Pritchard's desk. That made him feel uneasy because he had left the door unguarded, so he went back and wedged a chair under the doorknob. After that, he walked over to the teacher's desk and leaned against it, feeling that from here he had a better view of the class. That was when he glanced at the attendance register. It lay open at that day's date, with the newly-inked attendance ticks against the column of names. Idly, Dagget counted the ticks. There were thirty. Then he counted the children. Twenty-eight.

A small alarm-bell sounded in Dagget's brain. He counted the ticks again. Still thirty. Then he checked the date. Finally he counted the children again. Still twenty-eight.

Dagget picked up the register and slapped it hard against the side of the table to attract attention.

'Where are the other two?' he shouted.

Miss Pritchard stiffened. 'I don't know what you mean.'

'You know all right. Don't mess me about, lady. Thirty kids came in here this morning.

Now there are only twenty-eight. So where are the other two?'

'Oh, I see!' Miss Pritchard thought quickly. 'I sent one boy home sick, and another went with him. You don't send a sick child out alone.'

Dagget pointed at one of the boys in the front row.

'You! Is that right?'

The boy looked at Miss Pritchard, who stared straight back at him, chin held high.

'Yes, that's right.'

'If I find out anyone's been lying to me, the whole class is going to suffer.' Dagget pointed at another child. 'You! Who was sick?'

'Lenny Hargreaves.'

Dagget checked the register. 'Where's he live?'

The child he was questioning looked at Miss Pritchard, who gave an almost imperceptible nod.

'Number four, Pilling Street.'

'How far away's that?'

'Just by the railway station.'

'Right! We'll soon find out if he *has* gone home, and if he hasn't, then woe betide the lot of you.'

'You will not threaten these children!' cried Miss Pritchard angrily. 'I, and I alone, take responsibility for decisions made in this classroom.'

Dagget grinned nastily. 'Not now you don't, love!'

At that moment there were three sharp warning raps on the door—a prearranged signal—and Dagget had to hurry to let Stone in.

Stone looked very pleased with himself.

'Okay, that's it! Everything's in motion. All we have to do now is wait.'

'They'll send the helicopter and everything?'

'Haven't much choice, mate, have they?'

Dagget was so relieved he felt like hurdling over every desk in the classroom. It was all working out as Stone had said it would. It was actually happening! They were going to get away with it, and nothing could stop them now. Even the thought of the two missing children paled into insignificance. After all, the railway station was at least a mile away.

All the same, Dagget would have mentioned this to Stone if the next quiz question had not been punctuated by the sound of an approaching siren. The police were here. That thought drove all others from Dagget's mind.

5

It was dusty in the staff-room wardrobe. Lenny Hargreaves, huddled on the floor with an old fur bootee kicking him in the ribs, was in agonies trying not to sneeze. Luckily, since most of the staff were out there was only Miss Pritchard's coat in there, but a line of abandoned cardigans and sagging jackets hung just above the boys' heads, whilst all around them lay pairs of shoes in various stages of shapeless old age.

Jake had his eye to the crack in between the doors.

'Coast's clear,' he whispered at last. 'Shall we make a dash?'

'Where to?'

'Telephone.'

'No need,' Lenny pointed out. 'You heard him ringing somebody up. The whole world will know by now. That's the whole idea. He *wants* them to know, so that he'll get his ransom or whatever.'

'Well, we could escape out the back way.

Run home across the playing fields.'

'And leave Pritty and the others to their fate? Jake Allen, I'm ashamed of you!'

'I meant we could fetch reinforcements.' Jake was rattled because his courage was in doubt. 'You don't seriously think we can rescue them ourselves, single-handed?'

'Double-handed. We're the only chance they've got. The police will have all the reinforcements they want, but they can't do anything in case our kids get shot. But like I said, with the gunmen not knowing we're here, we could take them by surprise.'

'We'd have to have some weapons,' Jake retorted gloomily. Then he had a thought. 'Hey, suppose they've left more guns and stuff in the boiler-house? That's where they went first with those plumbers' bags.'

'I suppose it's worth a try,' agreed Lenny, edging the door carefully open and taking in a welcome gulp of stale staff-room air.

Slowly and cautiously the two boys crept from the staff-room down an assortment of corridors and out into the playground. After a final quick dash down a flight of stone steps they found themselves in the boiler-house.

'Dare we put the light on? I can't see a thing.'

'Yes, it won't show from the outside.'

Jake clicked the switch, and at once the two plumbers' bags were revealed in the middle of the boiler-room floor. But the bags were empty.

'Huh! Right waste of time that was! I don't suppose they'll even come back for these, so it's no use planning an ambush.'

Lenny began foraging around in a corner.

'There are plenty of weapons here, anyway.' He pointed out a shovel, a poker, a rake, some rope, an old football-net and a length of lead pipe. The shovel was so heavy he could only just lift it.

'What do you suppose we're going to do with those? We're nowhere near tall enough to bash anyone over the head unless they're lying down, and I wouldn't fancy it anyway. I'm a pacifist, me! Our best hope is to trick them. Use our brains, not our brawn.'

'All right then, you think of a trick!'

'A nice bit of magic, that's what we could do

with,' reflected Jake. 'Hey, what about one of your conjuring tricks or something?'

'You WHAT?' cried Lenny incredulously. Up to this moment, Jake Allen had steadfastly refused to have anything to do with Lenny's conjuring tricks, which he regarded with a mixture of amusement and scorn. Lenny felt both grateful and proud at this sudden change of heart. Now it was up to him to show Jake just how good he was.

At this point, Lenny remembered that all his conjuring stuff was at home.

6

Gun at the ready, Stone crouched by a corner of the classroom window, listening to the police loud-hailer blaring from the far side of the playground.

'All right, Stone, we've done as you asked. There's a helicopter on its way to pick up your friend and the money, then it will land on the playing field. It should be there in an hour and a half. So why don't you let those children go? We've got the vicar here, offering to come in as a hostage in their place. How about it?'

Stone sneered disdainfully. How soft did the police think he was? A classful of kids gave a lot better bargaining power than one middle-aged vicar.

For answer, he fired a single shot through the window, taking a notch out of a chestnut-tree in the front drive.

Fiona Crompton looked like starting to cry again, but Miss Pritchard hastily barked out a question she knew Fiona could answer and the moment of crisis passed.

'Team B are now leading by three points, thanks to Fiona, and I've got prizes for all those in the winning team, so the rest of you had better pull your socks up.'

Miss Pritchard had no idea what the prizes were to be, but no doubt she would think of something. The main thing just now was to keep the children's interest.

Suddenly an urgent hand shot up.

'Miss, please may I leave the room?'

There was an immediate flurry of hands.

'May I, Miss?'

111

'And me!'

'Me, too!'

Miss Pritchard glared defiantly at Dagget.

'Yes, of course, children. But one at a time . . . .'

Dagget, however, smiled and shook his head.

'No chance, lady! Nobody leaves this room except him and me. You've got a waste bin there. They'll have to use that.'

'I beg your pardon?' Miss Pritchard was outraged. 'They will do nothing of the kind! I never heard of such a thing!'

Dagget sighed patiently. 'If they want some privacy, pull that cupboard away from the wall and put the bin behind it.'

When Miss Pritchard began to protest some more, he snapped, less patiently, 'Look, missus, if that's the worst that happens to them, you'll be thanking your lucky stars before the day's out.'

'I wonder what *you* will be doing before the day's out?' reflected Miss Pritchard grimly. But she began moving out the cupboard, all the same.

Dagget nodded his approval. 'That's more like it! Your job's to do as you're told—and to keep these kids happy until the helicopter gets here. After that, you can call us all the names you like.'

'Stone!' the police loud-hailer rang out once more. 'We want a word with the teacher. Let her come to the window and talk. We need to make sure those children are all right.'

Miss Pritchard immediately stopped what she was doing and began moving towards the window, but Stone grabbed her arm and held her back.

'No luck, lady. If there's any talking to be done, I'll do it.'

'Have you no feelings at all? There are parents out there, wondering what's happening,' she began in an earnest whisper.

'Get on with your quiz,' advised Stone. 'Why don't you ask 'em how to spell "surrender"?'

7

Lenny could not forget what Jake had said about needing a touch of magic. If only his conjuring stuff had been available! He was sure he could have thought of something to distract the gunmen's attention long enough for them to be taken by surprise. And then he remembered something.

'Hey, Jake! There *is* some of my conjuring stuff here in school after all. Remember that imitation plastic pool of blood that I use for the sawing-your-thumb-off trick?'

'Oh, that!' Jake recalled. 'You were fooling about with it in class and Pritty confiscated it.'

'Right! So I'll bet it's still in her locker in the staff-room.'

Lenny was already on his way to look for this strange object when Jake asked:

'What use do you think that's going to be?'

Lenny began to explain, and Jake's face slowly brightened with hope.

'Hey, that's not a bad idea!'

It was certainly a daring scheme, but given a little luck it might just work.

'It's a case of do or die,' said Lenny. 'We haven't much choice, so we'd better get started.'

'You realise if it doesn't come off we could get shot?'

'It will come off,' Lenny assured him with all the confidence of the professional artist.

First they had to prise open Miss Pritchard's locker. They searched the staff-room for a suitable tool, and came up with a long, steel knitting-needle which eventually did the job.

'Great! There it is!' cried Lenny, rummaging in the locker and triumphantly lifting out the plastic dark red 'pool'. 'Now for that football-net we brought from the boiler-house. Just give me time to sort myself out in the cloakroom, then you go off and fetch help.'

Jake tried to swallow, but his mouth felt dry. He was suddenly very nervous. It was all right for Lenny Hargreaves, lying safe and snug on the cloakroom floor, but what about him, Jake Allen, having to go and tackle the gunmen face to face? He couldn't help wondering what it would feel like to get shot.

'Please let it work!' Jake prayed silently. 'Let them believe me, and I'll give up chewing-gum for ever.'

Then he took a deep breath and set off for Miss Pritchard's classroom.

Jake banged loudly on the classroom door.

'Miss Pritchard! It's me, Miss! Jake Allen. I can't open the door.'

This was not surprising, since Dagget had again wedged a chair under the door-handle.

Stone leapt from his place by the window, swinging his weapon towards the door. Dagget's face turned two shades paler as uneasy memories flooded back.

'It's all right,' said Miss Pritchard calmly. 'It's only the boy I told you about. The one who went off with the sick child.'

'What sick child?' Stone turned on Dagget. 'Did you know about this?'

'She said they'd gone home before we got here. Right to the railway station. I didn't think it mattered, so far away ....'

'In a job like this everything matters.'

Without relaxing his guard on the door, Stone spoke to Miss Pritchard. 'What's he up to, this kid?'

'Jake's come back to his class, that's all. He's not up to anything.'

'You never said he was coming back,' complained Dagget.

'I didn't think he'd bother, since it's the end of term, but he's evidently a conscientious boy. You'd better let him in. He can't just stand about in the corridor.'

'It's a trick!'

'Nonsense! He's only a child. Let me talk to him.' If Miss Pritchard could catch a glimpse of Jake she felt she would know at once whether he realised what was happening. If he did, she must warn him it was too dangerous to try to help.

'How did he get back into school?' Stone wanted to know. 'The police have this place surrounded. They wouldn't have let him in unless it was a trick.'

'Oh, dear! That serves me right for telling lies,' Miss Pritchard thought. Then Jake's voice came even more urgently from behind the closed door.

'Lenny's passed out, Miss. He's hit his head on the corner of the washbasin. He's unconscious, Miss, and he's bleeding like mad. I can't make him hear me. I've been trying for ages.'

'All right, Jake, just a minute!' Miss Pritchard turned to Stone. 'There's your answer. They never left school at all. Well, you'll have to let me go and see to the child.'

'There was nobody about when I went to the 'phone. I tell you it's a trick. That door stays fastened.'

'How can it be a trick? Do you think the police—our marvellous British police—would use a child like that? You can hear the genuine panic in the boy's voice.' Miss Pritchard, remembering suddenly what a great little actor Jake Allen had turned out to be in the last school play, confronted Stone with renewed determination.

'Look, there's a child hurt out there. He may be bleeding to death. You surely wouldn't

want that on your conscience? You pretend to be so keen on people's rights, trying to save your friend from punishment for a crime he didn't commit. All right then, what crime has that child committed? He needs medical attention, and I shall see that he gets it.'

The class watched tensely, silently cheering their teacher on. Miss Pritchard had gone up in their estimation quite a lot in the last half-hour.

'Get back, woman!' Stone held the teacher as she tried to reach the door. At the same time, however, he gave a signal to Dagget. Carefully,

Dagget removed the chair, inched open the door and poked his gun into the corridor. Then he kicked the door wide, snatched Jake's arm and dragged him into the room. The door crashed closed again behind him.

Jake Allen looked very upset, and his appearance caused quite a stir of interest in the class. Had something really happened to Lenny Hargreaves? And if it had, did that mean an ambulance might come and rescue them all?

Jake repeated his story about Lenny banging his head and lying unconscious, and ended with a dramatic plea for help.

'Aren't you going to *do* anything, Miss?'

'Of course we are, Jake. But for the moment this man's in charge. You must wait for him to decide.'

At last Stone gave in. 'All right,' he mumbled to Dagget. 'Go with the kid and have a look. Keep him right in front of you, just in ·case.'

'I'll go,' said Miss Pritchard quickly, not liking the thought of that gun at Jake's back.

But Stone only told her once more to mind her own business and get on with her quiz.

'It's all right, Miss,' Jake said courageously. 'He won't shoot me because I'm telling the truth. He'll be able to see in a minute.'

Jake and Dagget disappeared, and surely enough, almost immediately, Dagget's voice was heard calling back to Stone.

'It's okay, this kid *is* hurt, I can see him.'

Miss Pritchard, not knowing whether this was good news or bad, resignedly picked up the threads of the contest.

'Let's see—where were we?' She glanced at the blackboard. 'Team C. Danny, your turn. How many Ls in "parallel"?'

'Four, Miss. No, two. I mean—three.'

Meanwhile, Dagget advanced with some caution towards the figure lying in the pool of 'blood' on the cloakroom floor. Satisfied at last that this was a genuine emergency, he relaxed his hold on Jake and moved in to take a closer look at Lenny. That was when Dagget slipped on the soapy patch Lenny had laid on the floor beside himself. Before Dagget recovered his

balance or realised what was happening, there were two boys leaping round him, and he found himself struggling in the meshes of the football-net on which Lenny had been lying.

8

The two boys were luckier than they could ever have hoped to be. Fate took a hand in their capture of Dagget, for as the gunman struggled in the net, he swung his head with a mighty crack into one of the metal cloakroom posts and knocked himself out completely. It was an accident so similar to the one they had invented for Lenny that it seemed to the boys like poetic justice.

'I'll bet that was meant to happen,' said

Lenny with satisfaction. 'Jolly well serves him right.'

'Do you think we've killed him?'

'Not a hope! He'll be round in a minute, then he might kill *us*. Quick, grab his gun and let's tie him to the pipes.'

They made good use of the rope they had found in the boiler-house, and Lenny turned his tie into a gag. Jake obediently picked up the gun, holding it gingerly at arm's length. He didn't trust instruments of violence.

The two boys started back down the corridor.

'Mind what you're doing with that thing!' Lenny complained in a whisper as Jake accidentally prodded him with the gun. 'Here, you'd better let me have it. I know how to handle weapons.'

Lenny was referring to the toy pistol which was part of his conjuring programme. He would fire it into the air until a handful of loose feathers floated down, to the great amusement of the audience. Very effective, if you got it right, which Lenny rarely did.

Jake was glad to hand over the gun. He needed to concentrate on calling out again when they reached the classroom door. After all, Lenny couldn't call out, as he was supposed to be dying. But Jake need not have worried; the moment for him to call out never came.

What happened instead was that Lenny, tiptoeing right up to the door and preparing to station himself behind it, tripped over his own dangling shoe-lace, stumbled into the door and jarred his elbow. The gun went off.

Mercifully, the barrel of the gun was pointing upwards. The bullet sped through the thin plywood panel of the door and straight towards the adjacent wall, where hung the huge, magnificent, prize-winning collage. Stone had already heard noises in the corridor and had hastened to the door. Now he leapt backwards at the sound of the shot. He was just in time to take the full force of the collage board on the top of his head as Lenny's bullet loosened the plaster round the hook.

Stone sank with a groaning sigh as the great board sandwiched him to the floor—(Stone cold, as Lenny Hargreaves might have said)—and the gun he had been holding slithered away across the polish towards Miss Pritchard's feet.

Plaster-dust, screams and confusion filled the air. Chairs fell and desk-lids clattered as the frightened class took cover. As for Miss Pritchard, she bent down in utter disbelief and timidly gathered up the gun. As soon as she realised that Stone was in no shape to grab it back again, she grasped the weapon more tightly and marched determinedly to the door to tackle the second gunman.

'I'm armed!' she yelled, thinking that Dagget was in the corridor. 'So you'd better put up your hands!'

Carefully she drew back the door, and Jake Allen walked in with his arms obediently raised. Behind him stood Lenny Hargreaves, staring at his gun as if it had turned into a deadly serpent.

'Are you—alone, boys?'

'It's all right, Miss, the other one's tied up.'

This news snapped Miss Pritchard back into firm control.

'Right, Lenny, you'd better give that to me!'

Miss Pritchard now had a weapon in each hand, and wondered what on earth she was going to do with them. In the end she laid them both across her desk while she rummaged in her bag for a plain white handkerchief.

'Here, Fiona, shake this out of the window as a signal to the police.'

Then she picked up one of the guns again and pointed it vaguely in the direction of the prostrate Stone and the door. One couldn't be too careful.

9

All at once the classroom was full of policemen and shouting, bounding, laughing, crying children. Miss Pritchard's face turned quite grey and she sat down quickly.

The policemen were followed by ambulance men and nurses, who draped blankets over the children and led them outside, one by one, to the main gates where a crowd of parents, sightseers and journalists was waiting. Cameras flashed, mothers wept, bystanders cheered and reuniting families collided. In fact, the noise and confusion were even worse out there than they had been inside the classroom.

'Well done, boys!' Miss Pritchard managed to smile at Jake and Lenny, who still hovered anxiously at her side. 'But don't ever try a mad scheme like that again. Suppose you hadn't managed to hit the collage board? Or suppose you'd hit it and it hadn't fallen?'

'I wasn't trying to hit it,' Lenny admitted uncomfortably. 'It was all an accident.'

'We didn't think of anything so ambitious,' agreed Jake. 'We were just lucky, especially with the first bloke.'

'Well, it wasn't all luck,' argued Lenny. 'There was my plastic bloodstain . . . .'

Jake gave Lenny a kick on the ankle and quickly steered the subject away from the dangerous question of Miss Pritchard's busted locker.

'Pity we missed that helicopter, though. I'd have loved to see it come down on our playing field.'

'Too true!' agreed Lenny. 'We'll never get a chance like that again.'

The teacher was amazed. 'Don't you two

boys think you've had enough excitement for one day?'

Lenny treated this question seriously.

'It depends what you mean by excitement, Miss. There's scared-excitement and there's fun-excitement. Helicopters are fun.'

'Maybe we could get cut off by the tide or something in the holidays,' suggested Jake. 'Then they'd winch us up.'

Miss Pritchard was quite sure that Jake Allen and Lenny Hargreaves could manage a simple thing like that. However, she said she had a better idea.

'They run helicopter pleasure trips from Spagley aerodrome. Suppose I were to take you both up for a treat?'

'Honest, Miss?'

'Will you really?'

'As a sort of prize for catching the gunmen?'

Miss Pritchard gasped. 'Prize? Oh dear, I've just remembered. I promised prizes to the winning team in the quiz, but I haven't anything to give them.'

Lenny put a hand into his pocket.

'Don't worry about that, Miss. You can give them all tickets for my next conjuring show. It's in my dad's garage on Sunday afternoon. All proceeds for charity, including sales of chewing-gum in the interval.'

At these words, Jake Allen groaned and slapped a hand to his forehead.

'And *I've* just remembered I've promised to give up chewing-gum for ever.'

'Well now,' smiled Miss Pritchard, 'that is the most pleasing bit of news I've heard all day.'

3. The Vanishing Gran

Contents

1. Gran Vanishes   141
2. The Empty House   153
3. The Crime is Reported   166
4. Face to Face with the
      Criminal   174
5. The Flying Pennants   182
6. Emergency Help   187
7. Screams and Teaspoons   194
8. The Wanderer's Return   202

For my first grandchild
JOHN DEREK HINDLE
born June 4th, 1982.

1
Gran Vanishes

'You needn't think *I'm* having a baby-sitter!' cried Lenny Hargreaves indignantly. 'I'd rather swim the Channel in handcuffs and a ball-and-chain.'

Lenny's mother sighed.

'All right then, you'll have to go to your gran's for the weekend. I'm not leaving you in on your own, and that's that.'

Lenny's parents were planning a special

wedding anniversary celebration which involved a dinner-dance at the hotel where they had spent their honeymoon. Lenny had already refused to go along to that, but was now even more disgusted at the thought of having Marcia Herbert, from next-door-but-two, bossing him around for the whole of a Saturday evening. Why, she was only a few years older than Lenny himself. The whole thing was unthinkable.

Actually, the weekend at Gran's was not a bad idea. Lenny got on fine with her, and often felt it was a pity she lived so far away. But he wasn't going to give in just like that. He frowned and pondered. Then he said, as if reluctantly, 'Okay then – provided Jake goes with me.'

Jake Allen was Lenny's best friend. The two of them spent as much time as possible together, usually at Lenny's house since Jake had five brothers and sisters. The weekend would be a treat for Jake as well, and together they would really be able to make the most of it.

So negotiations started. Lenny's gran agreed

at once, but said it was a long way to come just for a weekend. Why didn't the boys stay for a week, since it would be school holiday time? Or even a fortnight, come to that? The scheme grew into a major expedition.

Lenny's dad, who was a long-distance lorry-driver, dropped the boys off at Gran's one Wednesday morning, promising to pick them up on his way back from Carlisle in a fortnight's time.

Gran Hargreaves's semi-detached cottage stood at the end of a country lane. On one side stretched open moors, and on the other side the lane wound down for a mile into a little village. The feeling of space was tremendous.

'We can make as much noise as we like at my gran's,' Lenny had already promised Jake; and in fact, on the strength of this promise, Jake had brought along his mouth-organ and a sheepdog whistle that he'd bought at a jumble-sale, neither of which he was allowed to play with at home. Lenny, of course, had brought his conjuring set. He was hoping to impress his gran with the latest 'Jumping Bottle', not to

mention the 'Multiplying Pennants' and 'Mysterious Message-slate'.

The boys piled out of the lorry and started off for the house, each clutching these most precious possessions, plus stacks of comics. Lenny's dad followed with the suitcases.

They found a notice on the front door of Gran's cottage, which said: GONE SHOPPING. BACK SOON.

'Sorry, lads, I can't wait,' said Lenny's dad, setting the suitcases down on the path. 'I'm late already. Have to be in Carlisle by half-past one.'

'That's okay, Dad. We'll mess about in the garden till she comes.'

'Yeah, well, not *too* much mess if you please! Righto then, see you in a fortnight. Be good, and give my love to your gran.'

Lenny's dad climbed back into his cab, reversed the lorry up the lane until he came to a turning place, then roared away with a last friendly wave.

After he had gone, the silence settled.

'Hey!' marvelled Jake. 'It *is* quiet, isn't it?

Bet you can hear the grass growing. Even the house next door's empty.'

'So it is!' Only now did Lenny see the FOR SALE board, swinging in the wind from a gibbet-like post in next door's garden. 'Wonder what happened to old Mr Gribble? Deaf, he was, and ever so forgetful. I'll bet he's had to go and live with his married daughter.'

'Great! Now we can make even more noise!' To prove it, Jake charged off round the lawn, emitting blood-curdling whoops and yells. Catching the fever, Lenny followed. Neither of them saw the startled face which peered cautiously out at them from a corner of one of next door's windows.

At last, they drew up panting and rosy-cheeked.

'Tell you what, I'm starving!' said Lenny. 'I could eat steak pudding, chips and peas, with apple pie and custard for afters and a bottle of coke to wash it down.'

'I could eat a pile of fat pork sausages and a great mound of creamy mashed, with beans in tomato sauce and chocolate cake to follow.'

'Let's have a wander round the back garden. We might find some raw carrots or strawberries or something.'

What they did find was a wheelbarrow, which immediately lured their thoughts from food. They began giving each other rides up and down the long path, then progressed to tipping each other out on to the grass. Finally, Lenny grazed his hands and decided he'd had enough.

'Hey, do you realise we've been here an hour and a half since my dad went?'

'I expect your gran's gossiping in the shops. My mum does that all the time.'

'Older folks ought to remember how hungry growing children get. Well at least I'm going in for a glass of water.'

'Isn't the door locked?'

'I know where the key is. See that little shelf in the back porch?' Lenny was already fishing out the back-door key and fitting it into the lock.

'Won't your gran mind us going in?'

''Course not. Anyway, it's her own fault. Back soon, she said, and now it's a quarter past two. I don't call that soon.'

The boys walked into the kitchen. On the table they found rows of freshly-baked buns on wire racks. The smell was delicious.

Lenny groaned. 'I wonder if she's counted them?'

He knew his gran would not mind if they took a bun each, but he felt that it would not stop at that. If the two of them once started on that batch of baking, they'd eat every crumb in sight. The only solution was total abstinence.

'Come on! We'd better go into the next room, out of temptation's way.'

But even here, the mouth-watering smell of baking lingered on. They had to do something to distract their minds from food. That was why Lenny fetched his conjuring set and asked Jake to help him practise his most ambitious project, 'The Vanishing Accomplice'.

'I've not really tried it out yet. I've only read up the instructions and that. You can be the accomplice and stand behind the curtain.'

149

Jake looked suspicious. 'What curtain?'

'We haven't got one yet, have we? Use your imagination. Here, stand by the window. As long as you're *behind* me, that's the main thing.'

Lenny set up his lightweight, folding table, re-read his instructions and began:

'Ladies and gentlemen, may I introduce my accomplice, Jake Allen, who has kindly agreed to assist me with this experiment? As you will presently see, I shall make him vanish completely.'

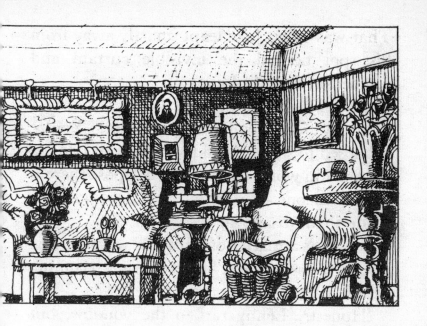

Jake wasn't worried. He knew Lenny's usual standard of trick. Feeling slightly bored and enormously hungry, he stood by the window as requested.

Lenny picked up his magic baton and waved it through the air.

'Now we close the curtain – so!' He whisked an imaginary sheet of material in front of Jake's face. 'Then I say the magic words:
"Zin, Zan, Zamba, Zin, Zan, Zeer,
Let the one behind me disappear!"'

That was when Jake leapt smartly away from his spot behind the invisible curtain and jumped in front of Lenny.

'Boo! I've disappeared!'

Lenny was really cross. 'Idiot! You're supposed to stay behind me. How can I do the trick if you won't co-operate? Suppose there'd been someone else behind me? I could have made them disappear instead of you.'

'Well, as a matter of fact there was someone else behind you. I just heard your gran coming up the path.'

'Honest?' Lenny ran to the window, but there was nobody in sight. The only movement he noticed was the gate blowing slightly in the wind. So of course Jake was mistaken . . . . Or was he?

2

The Empty House

Lenny's frown was both sulky and worried. He took his magic seriously and fully intended to make a career of it one day. He couldn't really have made his gran vanish, he supposed, but where was she? The whole journey to the shops and back should not take more than three quarters of an hour.

'It's time we went to look for her,' he decided. 'We'll fetch our luggage in, then walk

153

down to the village stores. We can help her carry the shopping. She always has to walk, 'cause the bus doesn't come this far.'

Jake groaned. 'It's a mile at least.'

'Do you good, a bit of fresh air and exercise.'

'On an EMPTY STOMACH?'

Lenny dragged in the last of the luggage, grabbed a couple of buns, then ushered Jake quickly outside.

As they began their walk, a furtive eye regarded them suspiciously from the bottom corner of one of next door's windows.

Apart from a rabbit which ran across the lane in front of them, the only moving things they met were birds. Not a human being in sight until they reached the village stores.

'Cox's Stores', however, was only too full of life. Lenny pushed his way into the crowd of shoppers and wriggled towards the counter.

'Excuse me – has Mrs Hargreaves been in today?'

Mrs Cox, the kindly owner of the shop, beamed over a box of apples.

'Yes, lovey, about half-past eleven. In a hurry, she was, on account of expecting her grandson. Here, that's you, isn't it? It's young Leonard, then! My, how you've grown!'

'Lenny,' insisted Lenny. (Goodness knew, that was bad enough, but Leonard – !)

'Well, your granny will be home long since. She said she was going straight back to make your dinner. It'll be getting cold by now.' Mrs Cox began to giggle. 'Oh, she hasn't half got a surprise for you!'

'But she's not there . . .' began Lenny, his voice drowned immediately by an impatient customer.

'Tell you what, I'll have four nice oranges, Mrs Cox. Oh, and how much is the boiled ham this week? Give me a couple of slices of that, then, love, and a pound of thin pork sausages.'

Lenny sighed. No use expecting help from this direction. He struggled out of the shop again, Mrs Cox calling distractedly after him, 'Be seeing you then, lovey. You'll be coming in for your toffees and that I expect.'

Lenny pulled a face at Jake, who was waiting outside.

'She disappeared between here and home over two hours ago.'

'Crikey!' Jake was impressed. 'She must be more of a magician than you. There's nothing between here and there except an empty lane. Maybe that trick of yours . . . .'

'You're forgetting something,' Lenny cut in sharply. 'There's that empty house next door. She must have gone in there.'

'What for?'

'I dunno. Feed the cat, or water the plants or something.'

'Empty, you said. No cat, no plants, nothing.'

'Funny thing is, I got the feeling there was somebody in there when we went past.'

'Here, just suppose – just suppose she *is* in there . . . as a prisoner?'

Lenny stopped. 'Kidnapped, or something?'

'Why not? Stranger things have happened, especially in my maths homework. Anyway, just think of Erica Carr.'

Lenny could not deny the strength of this argument. Erica Carr, who sat next to Lenny in class, had been captured by villains not so long ago, and rescued by Jake and Lenny. If it could happen once, it could happen again.

'Right, what are we waiting for?' Lenny started off at once towards the empty house.

'I'll just check my gran's again in case she's come home since we left.'

'Grab another couple of buns whilst you're at it.'

At last, fortified by further food, the two boys marched up the path next door and peered in at the front downstairs window. There was nothing to be seen except a thick layer of dust beyond the finger-marked pane.

'Looks a bit one-star.'

'Come on, let's try round the back.'

The garden was the same size and shape as Lenny's gran's garden, but there the resemblance ceased. This one was overgrown with knee-high grass and thistles, shapeless privet and clumps of fireweed. There were bits of blown-down roof-tile scattered on the path and a broken bottle on the back doorstep.

'My gran's not been here,' declared Lenny. 'She'd have picked up that broken glass, for a start.'

'Not if she was bound and gagged at the time. Hey, look! The kitchen window's broken.'

It was true. A whole pane of glass was missing. The gap had evidently been boarded up with a sheet of plywood, but this sheet now lay inside on the kitchen floor. Lenny leaned into the gap and peered around the kitchen. As he did so, a strange thing happened. A rosy apple, with a clean, white bite out of it, began to roll slowly across the floor.

Jake had seen it, too. The boys looked from the apple to each other. Then Jake nodded and Lenny started to climb quietly in through the gap.

It was not an easy climb. You had to step into the sink first, catching your shins on the taps. Then you had to sit on the edge of the sink, lowering your legs and launching yourself towards the floor. The water must not have been turned off either, for Lenny's seat felt decidedly damp by the time he'd arrived.

Lenny picked up the apple, his mouth beginning to water.

'Somebody's only just bitten into that.'

Even as he spoke there was a scuffling noise behind an inner door, followed by the sound of soft footsteps retreating rapidly upstairs.

'Kids!' sneered Jake, his courage renewed. He and Lenny bounded up the bare wooden staircase.

At the top, a bedroom door slammed in their faces. Someone was leaning on the other side, but the two boys soon managed to force the door open. When they burst into the bedroom they found, to their surprise, a solitary girl no bigger than themselves. She wore trousers and a thick jumper, though the day was warm, and her hair was gathered back in an elastic band. Her face was dirty and quite fierce-looking as she glared at the boys and said: 'I've not done anything wrong.'

'You're trespassing,' said Lenny.

'How do *you* know?'

''Cause my gran lives next door. This house belongs to Mr Gribble.'

'No, it doesn't, then. He died.'

'Well, it doesn't belong to you.'

'I've as much right to come here as you have.'

'We're looking for his gran,' Jake butted in. 'She's vanished.'

'Well, she's not the only one. What do you think *I'm* doing here?'

'You've run away from home? How daft can you get?'

The girl's cheeks turned pink. 'Why don't you two clear off and mind your own business?'

'You can't live here with no bed and nothing to eat and no fire or anything. You must be barmy,' decided Lenny.

'Anyway, somebody's sure to find you sooner or later,' added Jake. 'The house agent'll come. He'll be bringing people to look the place over, end even if *they* don't see you, somebody will buy it in the end and move in.'

'She could be the resident ghost,' grinned Lenny.

The pink cheeks turned to fiery red. 'I suppose you think only boys can do anything worth doing? Well, let me tell you I'm not half as soft as you think.' The girl leapt over to a

large fitted cupboard and threw open its door. Inside the cupboard was a sleeping-bag, plastic crockery and cutlery, a saucepan, a biscuit tin, a loaf of bread, soap and a towel.

'Hey, not bad!' Lenny was impressed. 'You could last a few days, at any rate. What did you run away for?'

'I'll bet it was your mum,' guessed Jake as the girl refused to reply. 'Do this, don't do that, don't answer back. If it was, you should take no notice. Everybody's mum's like that. You should hear mine on a Friday night when she's got five lots of hair to wash and the youngest two to bath and all the ironing for the weekend . . . .'

'What's your name?' cut in Lenny, who was only too familiar with the Allens' domestic scene.

'What's yours?'

'He's Jake and I'm Lenny.'

There was quite a pause before the girl said, 'I'm Jackie.'

'That's a boy's name.'

'No, it's not. It's short for Jacqueline.'

Lenny felt a sudden twinge of sympathy. Leonard and Jacqueline! Honestly, the grown-ups didn't deserve to win.

'How long have you been here?'

'As long as your nose!'

'Oh, don't be so touchy; we might be able to help you. Living next door, and that. We could save you bits of our meals.'

(If we ever get any, thought Jake).

Jackie relented. 'I only came this morning. But I'm going to stay for weeks. I'm going to give them a real good scare.'

'Yeah, if you say so. But it could be boring,

sitting up here by yourself all the time. Why don't you team up with us? You could help us find my gran.'

'She really has vanished.' Jake began the tale of the magic trick and all that had happened since.

'You mean your gran's that Mrs Hargreaves who lives next door? I've seen her this morning. A funny-looking man came and took her off in a car, if you call that vanishing.'

'You WHAT?'

'I told you she'd been kidnapped,' Jake said sadly. Now there would be no supper, either.

3
The Crime is Reported

'I don't suppose you noticed the make or the registration number of that car?' Lenny asked without hope.

Jackie's chin came up. 'As a matter of fact, I did. It was a dark blue Avenger, and I remember the letters because they spelt HAM. HAM 125T.'

Jake's face lit up with admiration. 'Hey, Jackie, that's great! We'll easily trace it now.'

Lenny, however, was looking suspicious. 'That came out a bit pat. You're not having us on, are you? Because if you are . . . .' Lenny left a threatening pause before he went on: 'We happen to know my gran went to Cox's Stores about half-past eleven. So how could she have been picked up in a car?'

'It could have been after she got home from the shop,' Jake pointed out.

'Then why didn't she take the notice down from the door?'

'Perhaps she didn't have time. He just caught her and whisked her off. Maybe he was just going to burgle the house when she walked in.'

Lenny grunted scornfully, but he was thinking hard. There was something in what Jake said. 'What time was it when you saw them?'

'My watch has stopped,' admitted Jackie grudgingly. Well, not even boys could make everything go right all the time.

Lenny gave Jackie a calculating look. Then he decided. 'Come on, then. We can't sit here.

We've got to catch up with that car. Come with us and identify it properly.'

'I've already identified it. What more do you want, the colour of the ash-tray?'

'Fair enough. Sit here by yourself in the dust, then, not even knowing what time it is. See you one of these days. Maybe.'

Lenny turned towards the stairs. Jake hesitated, as though he were going to speak to Jackie, then thought better of it and followed his friend. But at the last minute Jackie said: 'He was wearing blue overalls, and he had a great bush of black hair.'

'Sounds like a wig,' said Jake as he and Lenny struggled out by the kitchen window and started off down the lane.

Jackie did not follow, but watched them wistfully from the window. Then she picked up the bitten apple which Lenny had set down on the window-sill, polished it on her jeans and took another bite.

'We can't just hike around the countryside looking for a car,' grumbled Jake. 'It could be at John-o'-Groats by now.'

'We're going to the police station. It's that little house across from the church. There's only one constable for a village this size, and that's where he lives.'

Jake groaned, remembering another occasion when he and Lenny had tangled with the police. 'He won't believe us.'

'Yes, he will. They take things more seriously in the country. Anyway, he'll know my gran. Everybody knows everybody else round here.'

'You think that girl's telling the truth, then?'

'Yeah, I think she is, 'cause she knows if she's not we'll jolly well tell on *her*. Anyway, my gran's got to be *somewhere*. She wouldn't have left us with no dinner unless something was up. She's a great one for regular meals.'

The police station looked just like any other house, except for the POLICE notice over the door and the poster in the window showing a thief running off with an old lady's handbag. Lenny marched boldly up the path and rang the bell.

A woman in an apron came to the door, drying her hands on a towel. She was

accompanied by a toddler eating a jam tart, or at any rate pressing it to his face.

'Is the policeman in, please?'

'No, he's not,' said the woman, trying to guide the jam tart to the right bit of face.

'We wanted to see him urgently,' Lenny went on. 'It's about a missing person.'

'Could be a kidnapping, or something even worse,' Jake added with relish. Maybe he overdid the drama, for the woman's hand slipped and the jam tart skidded into the toddler's eye. The toddler howled with anguish.

171

'Oh, we know all about the kidnapping. (Hush now, Raymond, I can't hear myself think!) In fact the constable's gone off to Powerby now to help with the investigations. (Raymond, stop it! Now you've got jam all down my tights.) She's been spotted in Powerby, poor soul. Somebody saw her in a car with a man.'

'Yes, we know the number of the car.'

'You do?'

'And we've got a description of the driver.'

'Well, you'd best get in touch with the police right away. Best thing would be if you went into Powerby. They'll want to talk to you. (Oh, Raymond, go and get another one, then.). The Powerby bus will be along in a minute. Get off at the Odeon and the police station's only just round the corner. It'll only take you ten minutes. You got some money for your fares?'

'Yes, thanks.' Lenny jingled his holiday spending money in his pocket.

'Well, you tell all you know. Don't leave anything out. Because there isn't half a fuss going on over that poor dear, and I'm sure . . . .'

What the policeman's wife was sure of they would never know, for at that moment Raymond reappeared with a second jam tart upside down on his hair and the bus came into sight.

The bus had scarcely left the village behind when a strange thing happened. Jake, who was sitting next to the window, spotted a big, detached house standing well back from the road. Just inside the driveway of this house a car was parked. It was a dark blue Avenger, registration HAM 125T.

4
Face to Face with the Criminal

Never had two passengers disembarked so quickly from a country bus.

'That's not the Odeon!' the driver shouted, but our heroes were already gone. They had dodged between the gate-posts of this handsome house and were now cautiously homing in on the kidnapper's empty vehicle.

'This is a great place for a hideout,' whispered Lenny. 'Nothing for miles. We were lucky to spot the car.'

'I spotted it, and it wasn't luck, it was good management. Is she rich, your gran?'

'Nah! My dad's always wondering if she can manage on her pension. She does all right, though. She makes a bit of money painting pictures. Country scenes and that.'

'Wonder why she got kidnapped, then?'

'Perhaps she knows something. Perhaps she was sitting in the country one day, quietly painting a picture, when she saw a crime being committed. Or maybe she's been mistaken for somebody else. My dad says she looks like Mrs Thatcher in her best blue suit.'

'You never said she was an artist.'

'Well, she only took it up after my grandad died. Something to fill the time in, I expect. She says it's only a hobby.'

'What if she turns out to be famous, like Grandma Moses?'

'She won't turn out to be anything if we don't rescue her, that's for sure.'

'We can't just walk up the drive and knock at the door. He'll be watching. I'll bet he's got

binoculars. I'll bet he's watching us right now.'

'See that PUBLIC FOOTPATH sign? The path runs right along the side of the house. That's the way we'll go.'

'So that he'll think we're just a couple of kids out for a hike.'

'We'll saunter past the place and spy it out.'

Trying their best to look like happy wanderers without a care in the world, Jake and Lenny started off along the footpath.

'Point your arm in the opposite direction, as if we're interested in something miles away.' Distracting the audience's attention was something Lenny had learnt to do very early in his magical career. ('Let everyone concentrate on the empty cylinder you hold aloft in one hand, while you gently shake the coin down the sleeve of your other arm.')

As they drew level with the side gate of the house, both boys' hearts beat faster. What would they do if the kidnapper suddenly opened the door and came after them? Maybe they should have stayed on the Powerby bus after all, and left the tricky bits to the police.

'There he is!' Lenny grabbed Jake and pulled him down in the nick of time, as a black-haired man in overalls suddenly appeared in the back garden. Where had he sprung from? Surely he couldn't have been hiding behind the dustbin?

Now the man ran to the wall of the house, flattened himself against it and began to edge cautiously along towards the french windows.

'That's him all right! Did you ever see anybody act more like a criminal in your life?'

'If he's hurt my gran, I'll . . . !'

179

'Ssssh!'

Breathlessly, the boys watched as the dark-haired man in overalls gently undid the catch of the french windows, cast a hunted look around him and slipped indoors, leaving the windows slightly ajar.

Now the question was, should they go in after him? Lenny felt that if they went off to fetch help, his poor old gran could be minced up for cat-food by the time they got back. So maybe they should risk it.

Meanwhile, back in the late Mr Gribble's empty house, Jackie sat on her sleeping-bag and chewed miserably at a hunk of dry bread. It wasn't much fun. Maybe if she hadn't met those two boys the whole thing would have seemed more of an adventure, but after they had gone things turned very dull and boring. The trouble was, Jackie badly needed companionship, something absorbing to fill in the empty holidays. That was one reason why she had run away in the first place. All her pleas to be allowed to play with the farm family up the lane had been ignored, and there was nobody else for miles. After only two months she could tell she wasn't going to like living in the country. London had been much more exciting.

Jackie sighed and wandered back to the window. Where had Jake and Lenny got to now? Had they sorted out the business of the car? They were in the middle of a real adventure, and if only she hadn't been so proud she could have joined in. She could have made friends with those two. Jackie hacked off another hunk of bread, took a bite, then threw down the rest in disgust. Bread was horrible without butter and jam. Finally she came to a decision. Rolling her possessions up inside the sleeping-bag, she tied the bundle with string and started downstairs. She was going back home.

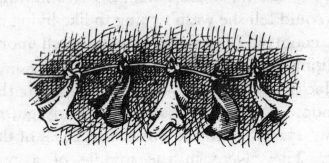

5
The Flying Pennants

'If we go in after him,' reasoned Lenny in a whisper, 'he could easily trap us.'

'Lock us up, you mean?'

'Lock us in with my gran. She'll be upstairs or in the cellar.'

'Well, suppose you go in, and I go for the police.'

One withering glance from Lenny put paid to that idea.

'You know the rules – always stick together in an emergency, and use your brains, not your brawn.'

'Go on, then,' urged Jake sarcastically.

'We'll try a bit of magic,' replied Lenny importantly. 'He's gone in and left the french windows ajar, so he's going to come out again. We'll catch him as he comes out. Take him by surprise.'

'Your magic stuff's all at your gran's . . .' began Jake, but he was wrong. Lenny was already drawing from his sleeve a bit of flesh-coloured tape which he handed to his friend. 'Here, take hold of this. Don't move from your side of the window, and don't let go whatever happens.'

Lenny ducked and ran to the other side of the french window. As he went, so the tape unwound from the depths of Lenny's sleeve, dragging forth little silk flags by the dozen, all in different colours. It was one of Lenny's favourite magic tricks, put on with his jersey this morning, which he had hoped to spring upon his startled gran at lunch. Jake lowered his end of the tape to the ground, as he saw Lenny had done, and crouched there waiting.

It seemed a long, uncomfortable wait. They could hear the kidnapper in the room beyond them, rattling cutlery as if preparing a meal. Jake almost groaned aloud with hunger, envying even Lenny's kidnapped gran if she was about to be fed.

Then all of a sudden, so that he almost caught the boys napping, the kidnapper made a hasty exit carrying a bulging haversack.

Lenny's end of the tape came swiftly up to knee height, Jake's end followed, the kidnapper rushed right into it and fell flat on his face on the path, festooned with coloured pennants like a royal visit.

'Sit on him!' cried Lenny, deftly demonstrating what he meant.

Their victim struggled, gasped and spluttered as Jake sank down on to his shoulders.

'What have you done with my gran?' yelled Lenny, bouncing up and down on the poor man's middle. Even if he had been able to

speak, the man would have had nothing to tell, for he had never even heard of Lenny's gran, much less kidnapped her.

Goodness knows what might have happened next if the two boys had been left alone with their victim. The man was not only strong but desperate, and had jerked the tape – (fastened to the inside of Lenny's jersey by a safety-pin) – so hard that the jersey had torn and was now unravelling at an alarming rate. Lenny could feel the draught growing stronger across his back.

But the situation was saved. At that moment a car drew up with a screech on the road outside the house. Doors slammed and running footsteps grew louder.

'Here come the police!' thought Lenny. 'And about time, too!'

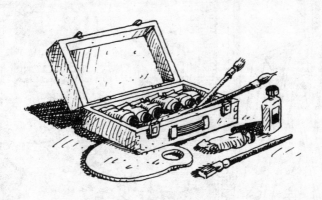

6
Emergency Help

Maud Hargreaves had taken up painting when her husband died, partly to fill in the time, but partly also because it was something she had always wanted to do. She bought herself an easel, a palette, canvasses, oil-paints and brushes, and began working away in the evenings with only herself to please. Then the vicar happened to drop by whilst she was finishing 'A View Across the Moors'. He was so

pleased with what he saw that he asked Maud to paint a similar scene for him, to hang in his study, where he could see it – and find inspiration – when writing his sermons.

Other people saw it, too. The vicar's visitors admired the painting, asked where it had come from, and eventually sought out Maud to order something for themselves. Then their visitors admired in turn, and Maud Hargreaves began to build up quite a reputation. She did not boast to her family about her accomplishment, partly because she could not believe that her success would last. She simply said she was happy with her 'little hobby'. And then, one day, she realised that she had sold so many pictures that she was getting quite rich. She decided to take driving lessons. If her son could drive a lorry all over Europe, surely she could manage a few quiet lanes for little country jaunts in summer? That way she would be able to find other, even more beautiful scenes to paint. Finally, after four attempts, she managed to pass her driving test. Then she bought a car – a second-hand, yellow Ford. Still she said nothing to her family, but arranged to have the car delivered on the day of her grandson's visit. What a surprise it would be for Jake and Lenny, and what fun for her to be able to take the boys out for rides!

Jed Soames from the garage – a lively lad with a great bush of black hair – spruced up the car for her and delivered it to her gate at half-past ten on the Wednesday morning of Lenny's visit. Maud climbed into the car and set off with Jed to drive him back to the garage. Next she called at the village stores and caused quite a sensation. Even the busy Mrs Cox came out to admire the vehicle, which Maud loaded up with shopping before starting out for some eggs at the nearest farm. So far, so good. Everything was working out to plan, and Maud felt excited at the prospect of astounding her young visitors.

Then things began to go wrong.

As she drove, Maud noticed the figure of a woman running distractedly along the roadside. Why, it was that nice Mrs Fox who had recently moved into the big house at the cross roads. Maud pulled up and wound down the window.

'Anything wrong?'

Mrs Fox turned a fearful, tear-stained face to Maud and began to pour out her tale of woe. Her daughter, Annabel, had disappeared.

'One minute she was in the garden, the next minute she'd gone. Somebody said they'd seen her drive into the village in a car with a man. The times I've told her never to take lifts from strangers! So I got into my car to chase after her, and my car wouldn't start. I tried to ring

my husband, but he's not in his office. So I've
just rushed out without thinking really, trying
to find out what's happened.'

'Here, you'd better get in,' Maud said
kindly. She had met Mrs Fox a few times at
church functions, and had thought her a
sensible woman. She wouldn't panic like this
unless there were a very good cause.

'We'll drive around for a bit and see if we can
find her. If not, we'll call at the police station to
report Annabel missing. Then I'll drive you
into Powerby to your husband's office. He'll

probably be back there by then.'

'Oh, Mrs Hargreaves, you're such a comfort! I don't know what I'd have done without you!'

Of course, Maud had not forgotten that her visitors were expected, but this was an emergency. There was a note on her door, and her visitors would just have to wait.

Maud and Mrs Fox drove around for quite a while, enquiring of everyone they met. Lots of people said they had seen Annabel, riding on a haycart, mending a bicycle, climbing a tree in the woods, buying ice-cream from a van, or playing hopscotch in the school yard with a couple of boys. All these stories had to be checked, taking time and getting nowhere in the end, which just goes to show that ordinary people have far more imagination than they are given credit for.

At last the two women realised they would need help. They told their tale to the village constable, who then went into Powerby with them to repeat the story and obtain instructions from his superiors. This took even more time, and it was well into afternoon before the women finally arrived at Mr Fox's office.

Mr Fox had just come in. He decided to abandon work for the day and take his wife home. So at last Maud was able to return to her visitors.

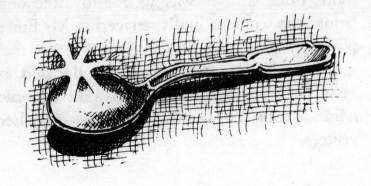

7

Screams and Teaspoons

Lenny was mistaken. The footsteps he had heard were not those of the police, but of Mr and Mrs Fox, who had just driven home from Mr Fox's office in Powerby. This house was theirs, and they had come home in obedience to police instructions, to wait for news of their missing daughter Annabel.

The first thing the Foxes heard was the commotion going on in the back garden. Was

Annabel already home? Excitedly, they ran round the side of the house – only to find a strange man lying face downwards on their path, swathed in coloured flags and topped by two dishevelled boys. It was a bewildering sight. Imagine going home yourself to such an unexpected welcome. Mr and Mrs Fox did not know what to think. But of course the disappearance of their daughter was uppermost in their minds, so when they heard Lenny yell something about a kidnapper, they immediately concluded that this man had made off with Annabel. Angrily, Mr Fox took charge. Sending his wife into the house to telephone for help, he seized the prostrate man and tried to shake answers out of him.

'What have you done with my daughter? Where is she? If you've so much as broken her fingernail . . . .'

Lenny's victim managed to wriggle his head free and gasp: 'Here, steady on! If you leave off shaking me, I'll try and explain. I don't know what I'm supposed to have done with all your blooming relatives – first his gran and then your daughter; goodness knows who it'll be next – but I haven't seen a soul all day till these two come along and tripped me up.'

Of course, Mr Fox didn't believe a word of this. Nor did Lenny and Jake.

'He was spotted!' yelled Lenny indignantly. 'Someone in the house next door saw him dragging my gran into his car.'

'They even got the number.'

'What car? I haven't *got* a car!'

'Take no notice of him!' Jake advised Mr Fox. 'His car's right there in your drive. You must have seen it.'

'Just a minute – !' pleaded the bewildered Mr Fox. But before he could say more there came a piercing scream from within the house.

'Annabel!' cried Mr Fox.

'Gran!' cried Lenny.

'Burglars!' cried Mrs Fox, rushing out of the house again in frightened indignation. 'We've been robbed, George! All the silver, even the teaspoons.'

'Teaspoons?' Lenny remembered hearing the clink of cutlery earlier on. Now he reached

out and pulled the haversack of the kidnapper towards him. It was stuffed with silver.

'I can explain everything,' the man began hastily. 'I'm just setting up a silver-cleaning service in this area, and you know how difficult it is to get a new business going these days. I thought if I gave everybody's silver a nice, surprise clean for free, then maybe they would . . . .'

'This is a nightmare! It isn't really happening!' muttered Mrs Fox faintly.

'What's all this got to do with Annabel, that's what I want to know,' cried Mr Fox, dragging the burglar into the house. Jake and Lenny followed, and although Mr Fox hadn't a clue who these boys were he felt it might be wisest to keep all the pieces of this puzzle in one place. Clearer minds than his would have to come and sort it out.

'There's no sign of Annabel here,' announced a distraught Mrs Fox. 'I've searched the house.'

'Don't worry, dear; we'll drag it all out of them in time. The police will be here soon.

Perhaps you'd better go and put the kettle on.'

Lenny felt suddenly uncomfortable. Mr Fox had said 'them'. It sounded as though he thought Lenny and Jake were villains, too. Jake, on the other hand, could only feel enormously cheered at the thought of the kettle going on. Maybe there would be biscuits to go with the tea – and possibly even a sandwich or a great, thick slice of fruit cake.

'Kidnapping,' said Mr Fox, 'is the worst crime in the book. In my opinion, no punishment is strong enough . . . .'

'Hear, hear!' interrupted Lenny. 'Especially when it's a poor old-age pensioner who can't defend herself.'

Mrs Fox turned at the kitchen door. 'A *what*? I honestly think I shall go mad quite soon. I have never lived through such a day in the whole of my life. George, will you tell me slowly, in words of one syllable if possible, exactly what has happened?'

George Fox took a deep breath. 'Well, dear, it seems this – this person stole your car to begin with . . . .'

'Then he must be a mechanical genius. I couldn't get the thing further than the end of our drive this morning. It just stopped and wouldn't start again.'

Jake turned wide eyes upon Mrs Fox. 'You mean – that's *your* car out there? That dark blue Avenger, registration number HAM 125T?'

Now it was Lenny's turn to feel confused. Was this lady his gran's kidnapper after all? If she'd disguised herself as a man, in overalls and dark wig, it was just possible. In that case, he and Jake had walked right into a trap. All this play-acting about burglars was just to put them off their guard.

'Well, it's time we were off now,' said Lenny, dragging Jake towards the french windows. But Mr Fox was there before him.

'Oh, no you don't! You're not going anywhere, my boy, until we've got all this sorted out.'

8

The Wanderer's Return

Tired and weary after her long trek from the village, Jackie reached home at last. Her feelings about this were mixed. There would be a lot of explaining to do, and she would probably get into trouble for running away in the first place. But maybe, after a little scare, her parents would see her point about needing friends. It wasn't so bad during term time, as she'd made a few new friends in school, but they all lived miles away and could only visit on rare occasions. There were boys at the nearby farm, but her mother had forbidden her to play with them.

Jackie sighed. Probably all she had done was to make her parents even more determined to keep an eye on her. Now they'd probably lock her in the house all summer. Miserably, she hitched up her bundle and turned in at the front gate.

Lenny saw her first as she came round the corner towards the french windows.

'Hey, there's Jackie!' As soon as he said it, the penny dropped.

'Jackie?' echoed Jake. Then he turned to Mr Fox.

'I'll bet your daughter Annabel tells whopping lies.'

Much later, when all the emotional fuss was over, Lenny complained: 'I wish you'd make your mind up what you're called.'

'I'm called Annabel,' the girl admitted, pulling a face. 'Only I think Jackie sounds a lot less soppy.'

'All right, I can understand that,' agreed Lenny, who had once thought of calling himself Alfonso after seeing a particularly exciting bandit film.

'But what about this car, then?'

Annabel's chin came up. 'It was your own fault. You shouldn't have talked down to me, just because I was a girl. You were so sure I wouldn't have noticed that car registration. I thought, "Right, I'll show 'em!" So I told you the first registration that came into my head. It happened to be my mum's.'

'Well, you'd no business to,' cried Jake. 'You've made us waste all this time now, and we could have been saving his gran's life.'

'Yes, she might have been put on a plane for Timbuctoo by now. If we'd gone straight to the police station as we were told, instead of following your false clue . . . .'

'Police?' echoed Mr Fox. 'Heavens, I'd forgotten all about them! I'd better ring them up and tell them Annabel's safe after all.'

'Don't forget about the burglar, George.'

Silence descended on the room as Mr Fox dialled the number. Then everyone listened in unashamedly to the nearest half of the conversation, which proved intriguing. Something else was obviously wrong. When Mr Fox finally put down the telephone, five faces turned questioningly towards him.

George Fox turned to the burglar.

'When you've finished your tea,' he said politely, 'I'll drive you to the station. Apparently the police have their hands full just now, so they can't come and get you. Two more kidnappings. Some woman just rang in to say her grandson and his friend had disappeared.'

Lenny turned pale, then pink.

'Hear that, Jake? My gran's okay!'

'We'd better get back for our dinner, then,' said Jake.

'I'd dearly love to know just what you have been up to,' declared Mr Fox, looking more suspicious than a donkey with a plastic carrot.

'Catching your burglar, that's what!' cried Annabel warmly. 'Not to mention persuading me to come back home. If it hadn't been for them, I might still have been missing.'

'We asked her to team up with us,' explained Jake.

'The offer still stands,' said Lenny generously. 'Could Jackie – I mean, Annabel – come back with us, please? My gran won't mind. We're here for a fortnight. She could come every day if she wants. She could come to our special conjuring session.'

'She could even be the Vanishing Accomplice,' Jake said happily.

4. Haunted Ivy

Contents

1. A Ghost is Born   211
2. The Ghost Vanishes   221
3. Spirited Away   228
4. Hole in the Ground   240
5. Bad News Travels Fast   245
6. A Strange Apparition   252
7. A Whirlwind Solution   262
8. Ghost Garden   270

For my 'BOOKLARK' colleagues:-
    Audrey Abel-Smith
    Eleanor Fidler
    Sue Goudie
    Christine Kloet
    Sheila Richardson
    Kathleen Ryan
    Derrick Scott
    Margaret Sumner
    Muriel Wills

1
A Ghost is Born

'What your Aunt Ivy needs is a ghost,' said Lenny Hargreaves to his friend, Jake Allen. 'That would pack the customers in.'

The two boys were slumped at a circular white table in the otherwise empty Ivy Tea Garden, miles from anywhere. All around them rolled acres of beautiful countryside, peopled solely by sheep.

The boys had previously spent a fortnight in

211

the country at Lenny's gran's, and both had enjoyed that very much. But then, Lenny's gran had a car and a sense of humour, and there had been other kids to play with in the village. Here, two miles from the nearest village of Bottlecombe, there was no one except Jake's widowed Aunt Ivy who had never been known to see the funny side of anything.

When he was first told that Jake's Aunt Ivy ran a tea garden, Lenny had visions of helping with mountains of washing-up. Once he had been assured that careful Aunt Ivy would never let him near her precious crockery, his mind then turned upon the interesting crowds of customers, for whom he could maybe put on magic shows while Jake took round the hat.

'I'm packing *all* my magic stuff,' Lenny told Jake, 'even the Vanishing Accomplice's special velvet curtain.' Since Lenny's dad, who was a long-distance lorry-driver, meant to transport them to Aunt Ivy's, there would be plenty of room for luggage. What could Jake do but sigh with resignation?

However, things did not turn out as expected. This was already the third day of the boys' visit, and the only tea garden customer so far had been a solitary hiker drinking a glass of milk with his own sandwiches, whilst he sorted out how he'd come to lose his way.

One thing was certain; Aunt Ivy could not be blamed for the lack of business. She was a genius in the kitchen, baked all her own scrumptious bread, cakes and scones, made her own jam, kept the place as clean as an operating theatre and tended every flower in her beautiful garden as if it were the vital stitch in the Bayeux Tapestry. Lenny felt she really deserved to succeed.

'It's a wonder your Aunt Ivy hasn't gone bankrupt. This place is too far off the beaten track,' mumbled Lenny, biting into a home-made raspberry tart with crispy, golden pastry. 'The main road must be three miles away. When you're whizzing down that at seventy miles an hour you're not going to stop for a two-foot strip of cockeyed board that says IVY TEA GARDEN NEXT LEFT.' He licked a stray blob of raspberry from his finger as he added:

'It's a rotten shame, this place going to waste. It needs a gimmick. Something to draw the crowds. Now, if that sign had a big, white picture of a ghost, and said HAUNTED IVY TEA GARDEN. . . .'

Jake sighed with exasperation. 'All you'd do with a ghost would be to scare Aunt Ivy off. She'd close the place down and go and live somewhere else.'

214

'Not if she started making a fortune. Did you ever meet a grown-up who wasn't interested in making money? Anyway, she'd know the ghost story wasn't true. She'd just keep quiet and rake in the cash.'

'You don't know my Aunt Ivy. She has a conscience. She feels guilty if she thinks she's forgotten to say good morning to the cat.'

Lenny Hargreaves rolled his eyes and

215

sighed. 'All right; she needn't even know. As long as we convince other people. We'll simply start a rumour that this place is haunted.'

'And just how do you think you're going to manage that?'

'Easy!' retorted Lenny after only the slightest hesitation. 'All we need is a big black umbrella—like that tatty-looking man's-size thing I saw in the hallstand. Then—you remember my "Digits in the Dark" trick?'

'The one where you have those painted numbers on a bit of black cloth and they glow when you turn out the light?'

'That's it! Well, all we have to do is open the umbrella and paint a face on it with that glowing paint. Then when it's dark we stick the umbrella out of our bedroom window and keep opening and shutting it. Anybody passing will think they're seeing a ghost, appearing and disappearing.'

'You reckon?' grinned Jake, entirely unconvinced. 'Well, there must be at least two people walking past here every week.'

'Alternatively,' Lenny cut in nastily, 'we

could just sit around here for the next fortnight and die slowly of overeating.'

There was a long, sulky silence. Then Jake unfolded his arms and said, 'Well, it's your idea, so you can go and ask for the umbrella.'

The paint-pot in Lenny's conjuring outfit was not very big. In fact, it looked more like an outsize meat-paste jar. Still, Lenny reckoned there was enough paint in it for a sizeable face. He cleared a space on the floor of the junk-filled garage, opened the umbrella and set to work, tongue sticking out and eyes screwed up in concentration. But Lenny Hargreaves was no artist, and the face took on a crazy, cross-eyed look which set Jake Allen laughing. Once Jake started he couldn't stop. He was soon lurching about the garage in helpless hysterics. He lurched so wildly that he collided with Lenny, who tripped over a rusty watering-can and spilt the paint all over the umbrella, completely covering up the face. Making a desperate grab, he tipped the umbrella over, so that the paint ran on to the inside as well.

Lenny was absolutely furious. 'Now look what you've done!'

'Well, honestly, if you could have seen. . . .'

'You've ruined everything now. There's no paint left.'

Jake sobered up. 'So what? No need to get so steamy. We can open and shut the umbrella just the same. It will look like a moving shiny blur from a distance, and that's just as ghostly. In fact, believe me, it'll be a lot more ghostly than that crummy face you painted.'

Lenny pretended to look hurt, but he was bound to admit that Jake was right. He only wished he had thought of the moving shiny blur himself in the first place. Still, the haunting was his idea. Any fool could mess about with the minor details of a plan, but the basic stroke of genius was what really mattered.

'Yeah, maybe it will work. We'll give it a try.'

''Course it will work. You just need to start people's imaginations off, and let them do the rest. You'd be surprised what eye-witnesses think they've seen.'

'You've changed your tune, haven't you?'

'Let's just say your enthusiasm is catching.'

'You realise we'll have to stay awake until midnight? That's when ghosts are supposed to show.'

'What if nobody is around to see it? That's the main problem.'

'There's a full moon tonight. With a bit of luck that umbrella will be visible all the way to Bottlecombe.'

'Well, if we have to stay up late we'll get Aunt Ivy to play Scrabble. It takes her at least half an hour to work out every move. I've known one game to last a fortnight.'

Lenny groaned. If there was one game he hated it was Scrabble. Too much like school, for one thing.

'All right, then. Leave the umbrella open to dry. We'll pick it up at bedtime.'

'The Haunted Ivy Tea Garden,' mused Jake experimentally.

'Sound great! If I was a sight-seer and I'd just heard about it, I'd be off there like a shot!' declared Lenny Hargreaves.

2
The Ghost Vanishes

During the evening a wind arose. The Scrabble game was punctuated by strange howlings under doors and inside chimneys, and a tree outside the kitchen window swung in growing frenzy against the glass. Perfect weather for ghosts!

Inside the house, the evening passed pleasantly enough, though spelling was evidently not Aunt Ivy's strong point. Lenny felt cheered

to find that there were other people as baffled by the English language as he was. Jake, on the other hand, had a flair for spelling and made the most of it. None of this turning soft and letting the others win a game, just to keep them happy. Yet for once Lenny Hargreaves did not mind losing. He had his haunting to look forward to.

By the time the boys went off to bed it was almost eleven o'clock. Swift, black clouds chased over the moon, leaving only occasional patches of light.

'You go upstairs and start making a noise in the bathroom,' whispered Lenny, 'whilst I nip round to the garage to collect the umbrella.'

It would never do for Aunt Ivy to guess what they were up to.

But when Lenny reached the garage, he had his first shock of the evening. The umbrella was not there. At first he thought Aunt Ivy had closed it up and tossed it among the other junk. Or had she put it back in the hallstand? After a great deal of frenzied searching, Lenny stormed upstairs.

'All right, what have you done with it?'

It turned out that Jake had moved the umbrella outside the garage door, to help it dry more quickly in the fresh air.

'Fresh air's right, you nutcase! Only it happens to be a force ten gale. That umbrella's probably blown to Timbuctoo by now.'

'Well, it was a crack-brained scheme to start with.'

'You're useless, you know that?'

'At least I can *spell*.'

'Big deal!' grunted Lenny, climbing disgustedly into bed without even cleaning his teeth.

Halfway to a dream, however, he was roused again by a frantic knocking downstairs. Aunt

Ivy had a customer!

'Hear that?' Both boys sat up in bed.

'It's after midnight. Something must be up!' United by a crisis, they were instantly friends again. As one, they leapt out of bed and rushed to listen on the landing.

Aunt Ivy, who had just been locking up before retiring for the night, was now unbolting the front door again, though she kept it on the chain as she peered through the gap and asked who was there.

'It's me, Dave Doyle!' a man's voice called. 'Do you mind if I come in and use your 'phone?'

'He's from the farm up the lane,' whispered Jake. 'His own 'phone must be out of order. Perhaps the lines have blown down.'

'Well, he's no need to make such a noise about it.' Lenny was thinking wistfully that here would have been the perfect ghost-spotter, if only they hadn't gone and lost the ghost. How maddening! He was about to trail disappointedly back to bed when he had the third shock of the evening, hearing what Dave Doyle was saying as Aunt Ivy let him in:

'Have you seen it? Isn't it amazing? I couldn't believe my eyes, honestly. I just stood and stared at it like somebody daft. Going to ring the papers right away, before it's out of sight. They pay you for stories like this, you know, and by the time I get home it could be gone.'

'What could be gone? What are you talking about?' Aunt Ivy followed Dave to the telephone, sniffing suspiciously at his breath, but she did not learn any more until he had dialled his number.

'*Bottlecombe Bugle*? Dave Doyle here, Lane End Farm. I've got a scoop for you if you're interested. There's a FLYING SAUCER hovering over the Ivy Tea Garden right this minute. No, not sorcerer; *saucer*. As in tea-set. No, I haven't been celebrating. If you must know, I've been to a Temperance Meeting. All right, if you don't believe me, grab your binoculars, walk outside and look up!'

Jake and Lenny waited to hear no more. Despite the fierce wind, they flung open the landing window and thrust their heads out into the night. The wind was deafening. Dustbin lids and milk bottles bowled around the back garden, whilst from further afield came louder bangs and rattles, as gates, sheds and fences took the strain. The boys were just in time to see a curved silver shape disappearing swiftly but gracefully behind the farthest clump of trees in the nearby wood.

'Our umbrella!'

'Fancy thinking that was a flying saucer!'

'I told you folks would believe anything!'

'Even ghosts, then.'

'Yeah, what a waste!'

'Oh, I dunno! This could be a stroke of luck.' Lenny began dragging Jake back into the bedroom. 'This could turn out as good as any ghost. If the flying saucer tale gets into the papers, everybody will want to come and look at the place. And while they're looking they can be stuffing themselves with your Aunt Ivy's coffee and scones.'

'Huh! There won't be much of a story left when they find that umbrella!'

'They're not *going* to find it!' Lenny was already scrambling into his clothes.

3
Spirited Away

Jake and Lenny stood on the edge of the wood and peered into the blackness. 'It can't be in there,' grumbled Jake. 'It would never have come down through all those trees.'

'Well, it's not on the outside of the wood, either. Must have caught on a treetop.'

'It might have taken off again. Didn't somebody mention Timbuctoo?'

'No, it didn't take off again. We'd have seen

it. It's around here somewhere.'

'All right, let's walk back up the fields in case we missed it.' Jake suddenly stopped and held out his hand. ''Course, it would blooming-well start to rain!'

Lenny was growing crosser every minute. The loss of the umbrella was all Jake Allen's fault, yet the lad did nothing but grumble and complain. The final straw came when Lenny's torchlight suddenly flickered and died.

'Huh! That's all we need! Here, shine your torch this way, so I can see what's up with mine.'

'Needs a new battery, that's all. Didn't you bring any spares?'

Lenny fiddled about with his torch wondering if it might help to bonk Jake on the head with it. Now Jake would have to be leader. As if that wasn't bad enough, it was Jake who suddenly claimed to have spotted the umbrella.

'Look! It *is* in the wood, after all.'

Certainly there was a round, shiny shape bobbing merrily about among the trees. Was it their umbrella? Lenny could hardly believe it.

'How did it get in there?'

'Perhaps it blew in along the ground. Let's grab it before it blows away again.' Stabbing his torch into the darkness, Jake leapt in among the trees, leaving Lenny to stumble and blunder behind him.

It was incredible how difficult the going suddenly became. There were roots and tangles everywhere, and long, sharp, nasty twigs that tried to scratch the boys' eyes out. Every step required concentration; it was no use trying to hurry. Even at the slowest pace, there were untold hazards. At one point, Jake caught his foot in a rabbit hole and stumbled forward on to hands and knees. The torch flew from his grasp and rolled down a bank, where it settled snugly into a clump of bracken. A good thing the beam of light was uppermost, to guide Lenny to where it lay. When Lenny came back from his scramble down the bank, he found Jake hopping crazily up and down.

'I've lost my shoe.'

'How have you managed that?'

'It came off when I fell.'

'You prize idiot! Why didn't you stand still, then, until you found it? Now you've gone hopping about all over the place we'll never know where it is. Here, let me look.'

Lenny shone the torch around in all directions, but there was no sign of the shoe.

'Whereabouts were you when you fell?'

Lenny had lost his own bearings because of the scramble after the torch, and all Jake knew was that it was most uncomfortable to put his shoeless foot down on the prickly wet ground. As for the umbrella, they had now lost sight of that completely.

'Oh, let's pack it in! We'll come back in the daylight.'

'Somebody else could have found the umbrella by then.'

'So what? Nobody's going to believe that tale anyway. I'll bet the *Bugle* editor's laughing his head off this very minute.'

'You were the one who said folks believed anything.'

'That was before I lost my shoe.'

Lenny sighed, suddenly realising how tired he was, not to mention scratched, wet through and fed up. 'Can you make it home with only one shoe?'

'I'll manage. But my mum's not going to be overjoyed at forking out for a new pair.' Wearily they turned in what they thought was the right direction for Aunt Ivy's. But they were in for a shock. The tiny pathway suddenly seemed to peter out, and the trees had grown ominously darker and closer together. Feeling uneasy, the boys forged anxiously ahead, getting ever more tangled in the thickening undergrowth. Half an hour later, they had to admit they were lost.

Meantime, at the Ivy Tea Garden, the excitement was building up. Mr Grubb, the *Bugle* editor himself, arrived by car, having insisted that Dave Doyle should wait for him there, on the spot where he had sighted his saucer, rather than go rushing off home.

'Now then, Dave, what sort of a tale is this supposed to be?' Mr Grubb looked decidedly

sceptical, though he had his notebook with him all the same.

'Didn't you see it? I know it sounds crazy; *I* couldn't believe it either, but it was there all right.'

'It was probably a plane you saw, or a helicopter.'

'Too low; far too low.'

'Maybe it was in trouble. We could 'phone the police and see if there's been a crash in the area.'

'We'd have heard a crash,' insisted Dave

quite crossly. 'Anyway, I tell you it wasn't a plane. It was round. A proper circle. Looked more like a giant frisbee than anything.'

'Now, let's not get carried away,' cautioned Mr Grubb, trying hard not to smile. 'Facts, we want, not wild flights of fancy.' He turned to Aunt Ivy. 'Didn't *you* see anything?'

Aunt Ivy had to admit that she had just caught a glimpse of something silver disappearing over the treetops as she opened the front door, but surely to goodness it could not have been a flying saucer? There were no such things.

'I wouldn't be too sure about that if I were you,' Dave said darkly. He had just been reading a book by an American who claimed to have talked to two Venusians in some desert or other. 'If we can reach the moon, then why shouldn't other beings get to us?'

Mr Grubb surveyed the night sky carefully. 'Well, there's nothing up there now except a load of rain-clouds. We'll leave it until the morning and see if any reports turn up from elsewhere.'

'That means you don't believe me. Well, you'll be sorry. When did your paper last have a decent bit of news in it?'

'Why don't we all have a nice cup of tea?' offered Aunt Ivy, trying to keep the peace. She began arranging crockery and biscuits on a tray.

'Just a quick one, then.' The editor looked at his watch, reminding himself that he still had that morning's stamp and postal-order snatch at Bottlecombe Post Office to write up.

There was a piece of news, all right! Mr Grubb intended to give it a whole front page spread. That would make Dave Doyle eat his words, and no mistake!

It was as Aunt Ivy was crossing the hall with the teapot that she noticed a strong draught blowing in from the staircase. The landing window was open! Strange. She could not remember opening it, and surely the boys would never do such a thing on a windy night like this? Having delivered the tray to her guests, she went off upstairs to investigate. First she closed the landing window. Then she

noticed that the door to the boys' room was open. She peeped inside—and found them gone! Their beds had been slept in, but the boys were not there. Alarmed, she dashed from room to room, finding no trace of the boys except a dirty sock on top of the bathroom cabinet. Finally she burst in upon her guests with the shocking news that her nephew and his friend had vanished!

The editor's whole face lit up like a Christmas tree.

This was more like it! A real, down-to-earth mystery that could share the front page with the Post Office drama. Two good stories in one edition; it had never been known before. Mr Grubb whipped out his notebook again and started firing questions; Aunt Ivy was distraught.

'You don't suppose it has anything to do with—what Dave was saying?'

Into her mind swam a picture of the boys being spirited away through the landing window by some fantastic machine belonging to aliens from outer space. Crazy, the way your imagination ran away with itself when you panicked. She could now understand Dave's story much better than she had done half an hour ago.

'I'm sure there's a simple explanation,' soothed Mr Grubb, hoping otherwise. 'Best thing we can do is to search around outside. Then, when we're sure they're not just hiding or playing a game, we'll get on to the police.'

'Police?' shrieked Aunt Ivy.

'Only to help us search a bit quicker. They

know how to set about these things properly.'

. 'It's all my fault!' Aunt Ivy wailed. 'I should have made sure the landing window was locked. I should have....'

'There, there!' Mr Grubb gave Aunt Ivy's shoulder a consoling pat. 'I'm sure it will all end happily.' As far as he was concerned it would, for he had just thought of a wonderful headline: MISSING BOYS IN UFO MYSTERY. It was the best thing that had happened to him in years.

4
Hole in the Ground

'I'm not going any further,' declared Jake Allen, standing on one leg with his weight against a tree. The sock on his shoeless foot now had more holes in it than a hairnet.

'I don't blame you. It's bad enough with two shoes on.' Lenny's own two shoes were packed with mud, inside and out.

'We'll have to sit here until daylight, rain or no rain. I refuse to fight my way through any

more branches.'

'I'll have a scout around. There must be a bit of shelter somewhere. Lend me your torch a minute.'

'Not likely! You're not going off and leaving me in the dark.'

'Don't be so soft! What are you scared of—a pack of ravening wolves, or the Abominable Snowman?'

'Suppose that bobbing shape we saw wasn't the umbrella after all? We never caught up with it. It just seemed to disappear.'

'Oh, come on! You don't think it was a real ghost, do you?'

'It's all right for you. I can't even run away, my foot's so blooming sore.'

'You won't have to run away. I'll only be gone two minutes.' Lenny took the torch and swung it in a wide arc, peering hopefully into the night.

At last he called: 'There's a great slab of rock over there. I'll just see if we can crawl in underneath it.'

'Don't go and get stuck or anything.'

Lenny shuffled off and returned almost immediately with the news that he had found a neat little hollow. 'Like a sort of cave. It'll be great. There's a big slab of rock to sit on, and an even bigger one hanging over it to keep us dry. It's even got creepers hanging down like curtains in front of it. Come on, I'll show you.'

Jake hobbled after his friend, and was relieved to find that Lenny's promise was true. He sat down with a sigh of exhaustion. 'I couldn't have gone another step.'

'Not exactly five-star,' admitted Lenny, 'but it will have to do until morning.'

'I hope Aunt Ivy hasn't missed us, that's all.

She'll go frantic if she has.'

'She'll be snoring away by now.'

'I wish I was. You and your dratted ghost.'

'If you hadn't left that umbrella outside. . . .'

'And if you hadn't brought your magic stuff on holiday, especially that crummy luminous paint . . . .'

They went on sniping at each other, with less and less energy and conviction, until both of them fell asleep.

It was almost two in the morning by the time Constable Waddle arrived at Aunt Ivy's on his bicycle. The constable had not managed more than ten minutes' break, he said, since the Post Office drama, so he was not feeling too good-tempered. The garden and surrounding fields had been searched by Dave Doyle and Mr Grubb, but the boys had not been found. Aunt Ivy was in a state of great agitation.

'Can't do much till daylight,' pronounced the constable. 'It would be hopeless, groping round in the pitch dark and all this rain. It's only a couple of hours to dawn.'

'We can't wait for dawn!' Ivy cried in horror. 'Goodness knows what could happen to those poor boys while we're sitting here doing nothing.'

With a sigh, the constable began to explain the difficulties of setting up a search-party, and in fact, since there were two boys missing instead of one, he was not yet convinced the matter was urgent. They were probably off on some secret assignment of their own.

'I don't mind driving around for a bit,' Mr Grubb offered. 'I could go up as far as the edge of the moors. Just let me make another couple of 'phone calls first.'

He smirked with satisfaction as he thought of his sub-heading: ALL NIGHT MOORLAND SEARCH—EYE-WITNESS REPORT.

5
Bad News Travels Fast

The television van arrived soon after dawn. It pulled up outside the Ivy Tea Garden, blocking the narrow lane and looking totally out of place in such rural surroundings. Two young men emerged from it and stared thoughtfully over Aunt Ivy's garden wall. One of them consulted a clip-board, then walked up the path and rang the doorbell, whilst the other sat down on the wall and lit a slim cigar.

Minnie Doyle, Dave's wife, who had been summoned to keep Ivy company, opened the door.

The man with the clip-board said good morning and wondered if it were too early for breakfast.

'We're closed!' Minnie told him brusquely. She had been up all night and was feeling the effects. But before she could shut the door again, the man slipped his foot into the gap and beamed up a charming smile.

'This is Bottlecombe's Ivy Tea Garden, isn't it?'

'Can't you read, then?' Minnie had no time this morning for social niceties. She was concerned only with poor Ivy's welfare.

'We're investigating a couple of possible items for tonight's regional news programme, and of course we need to make an early start. I'm sure you won't mind if we. . . .'

'Oh, yes I will mind! We aren't open to nobody today, not even if the Queen herself was to ask, so you can just go and do your investigating somewhere else.'

The man found this an unusual reception. Most people were only too keen to get themselves on to a news programme. Still, nothing daunted, he raised a hand to the second man, who rose from the wall and joined him. Introductions followed. Minnie heard the men's names as Jostling and Orbury, and was not impressed by the smoke from the slim cigar, which she wafted vigorously aside.

'Just a couple of questions, that's all,' smiled Orbury through his smoke haze. 'Then maybe two or three shots of the place. . . .'

'Shots, is it? Well, let me tell you my dad's the gamekeeper in these parts, and if there's any shooting to be done, he'll do it. If you're not off this doorstep in ten seconds flat. . . .'

Orbury, to his great disappointment, was never to savour the full richness of Minnie's threat, for at that moment Aunt Ivy herself appeared in the doorway, haggard and haunted-looking, but as gentle-voiced as ever.

'It's a bit early for sitting outside, but if you'd like to come into the kitchen I'll make you some coffee in a minute. Then I could do you ham, eggs, tomatoes, toast and marmalade.'

Minnie was indignant. 'Ivy, you can't!'

'Why not? Life must go on. I'd rather keep busy until the searchers get back, and anyway these gentlemen may be able to help. If they put it out on the news that the boys are missing, maybe somebody, somewhere. . . .'

Tears rushed into Aunt Ivy's eyes and she could say no more. Minnie flew protectively towards her, at the same time rounding on the intruders. 'Now look what you've done! You ought to be ashamed of yourselves. You're worse than them newspaper folk, and that's saying something.'

Both men began to apologise at once. 'We didn't know anything about missing boys.'

'You'll have to forgive me,' Aunt Ivy smiled bravely. 'I know the boys will turn up soon with some simple explanation. Boys that age are full of mischief, especially our Jake's friend. It's just the waiting—and all these funny rumours.'

'Ah, yes!' Jostling hoisted his clip-board. 'That's what really brought us along. These rumours. Somebody is supposed to have spot-

248

ted a UFO, I believe?'

Minnie gave Ivy a gentle push towards the house. 'You go and see to the breakfasts, then. I'll deal with the rumours.'

As soon as Ivy was out of earshot, Minnie spoke sharply to the men.

'Can't you see she's upset? You don't want to go making things worse for the poor soul. The policeman's got a search-party going, so why don't you set off after them? They've only just left here, and they're heading for the woods.'

'We really wanted to talk to an eye-witness about this UFO.'

'That's my husband, Dave Doyle. He's gone off with the search-party. You can't miss him; he's wearing a blue anorak and a blue corduroy cap. He'll tell you a tale, all right. In fact, you'll have a job to stop him. You can believe him, an' all, for he hasn't the brains to make up a tale like that. If he says he saw a flying saucer, then he saw one.'

Jostling looked at Orbury. 'What do you think?'

Orbury shrugged. 'Not much doing at all,

I'd say. Maybe the missing boys are worth a line or two. Couple of shots of the search-party, something like that. After breakfast, of course.'

'Odds are these boys will have turned up again by then, so we won't be able to use the story.'

'Oh, you never know your luck!' smiled Orbury hopefully.

6
A Strange Apparition

Lenny Hargreaves woke up with a start. Something small and furry had just run over his foot. Heart beating fast, he fought a double battle with his memory and his cold, stiff limbs, as he tried to scramble to his knees. Then it all came back to him; the umbrella, the search, the lost shoe and the hiding-place.

'Hey, Jake! Wake up, it's coming daylight! We can try to find our way back now.'

'Uh?' Jake rolled over sleepily, then suddenly started groaning. 'Ooooh, I think I've got rheumatics, like my grandad.'

'Now we know what the chickens feel like in the deep freeze.'

'I'll never walk again.'

''Course you will! You just need to get your circulation going.' As they crawled out of their hiding-place they saw immediately that the wood by daylight was a much friendlier place. The rain had stopped, the birds were singing, early sunlight filtered sideways through the trees.

'Try this!' Lenny began swinging his arms and running on the spot, but Jake's effort looked more like a limping gorilla. When they had limbered up sufficiently, they took stock of their surroundings.

'Which way do you think we should go?'

'Haven't a clue! Unless—wait a minute! That's my shoe over there!'

Jake lumbered forward to gather up this soggy object, whilst Lenny groaned in disgust. 'We must have gone right round in circles then,

last night.'

Jake thrust his toes into the shoe. 'Ugh! I think there's mushrooms growing in it.' He tipped up the shoe and shook it. A leaf fell out, then a small, black, squashy lump. 'That's better! Now let's get back home. I'm starving.'

'Yeah, three-and-a-half cheers for breakfast! I'll have four eggs, five rashers of bacon, six sausages, eight rounds of toast and ten cups of tea,' Lenny threatened.

'By then it will be time for elevenses. Hot buttered scones with raspberry jam, raisin pancakes, cream buns and coffee.'

254

'No, milk-shakes.'

'Hey—I've just remembered something. It's apple crumble day!'

Spurred on by the thought of all this food, the boys made splendid progress through the wood. They soon found the path again, and were nearing the stile that would lead over the last fence into the fields beyond when Lenny halted, staring goggle-eyed before him.

'Look at that!'

'What is it?'

'Looks like—a FLYING SAUCER!'

The boys gazed spellbound into the field beyond, where a great silver upturned basin sat strangely upon the grass. It was big enough to mix an omelette that would feed five thousand folks.

'We're not dreaming, are we?'

'You pinch me, and I'll pinch you.'

'Dave Doyle was right, then. What he saw was nothing to do with our umbrella.'

'Looks like it.'

'Hey—don't you think it's a bit spooky?' asked Jake.

Lenny grinned. 'It will be if we hear any little green men shouting, "Take me to your leader!" Apart from that, I'd say it's more interesting than anything. It's not every day you see a sight like this.'

'Intriguing, that's the word for it,' Jake offered, showing off.

'No kidding? I'll bet you can spell that, can't you?'

Lenny was already crossing the field towards the flying saucer, so of course Jake followed him, though he managed to keep well in the rear. He wasn't scared, he told himself; just cautious. Nobody could accuse Lenny Hargreaves of that.

Lenny stared hard at the object, taking in every detail. It seemed to be made of a sort of lightweight, shiny plastic, though of course it could be some special space-substance, never seen on earth before. Lenny willed it to be a genuine UFO, though well aware that Fate was rarely so obliging. Just suppose it were, though? What an adventure to tell when they got back to school—if they ever did!

The boys circled the saucer cautiously, discovering a broken place at one side of it, near to the base of the curve. (Had a meteor hit it?) So of course Lenny had to stick his head inside the hole.

'There's something in there, making a noise. Trying to communicate with us.'

'Sure to be!' sneered Jake, but his stomach gave a peculiar lurch and he looked round for a suitable weapon, just in case. There was a blown-down branch nearby, so he picked that up and tried a few martial arts manoeuvres. Lenny started laughing.

'You know what it is? It's a cat! Daft thing's jumped in and can't get out. We'll have to rescue it.'

'You're not going in?'

'I think I've a bit more sense than a cat.' Lenny had already put one foot through the gap.

'You haven't got nine lives.' Jake's imagination had filled with banks of computers, flashing lights and electronic beams. As for the actual life-forms that might be in there. . . !

Shouts and cat noises began to echo round the dome, and once or twice Lenny screeched with pain. At last he caught the animal and held it up towards the hole. 'Catch!'

The cat, thoroughly scared, writhed energetically in Lenny's grasp and finally leapt away, right over Jake's outstretched arms, to run off down the field as if all the Dogs of Mars were after it.

'Hasn't half scratched me!' complained Lenny, lifting red-streaked hands on to the edge of the gap. 'Here, help me out.'

'What's that you've got?' Jake was staring at a bundle of papers stuffed into the front of Lenny's anorak.

'Taped to the roof, these were. Secret documents from outer space. Wait till the *Bugle* editor casts an eye on this lot!'

'They're sheets of postage stamps!' Jake had noted the neatly-perforated edges. Lenny took out the bundle and examined it more carefully.

'You're right! Stamps—and postal orders!'

'Perhaps the Daleks do football pools,' sneered Jake, throwing down his stick.

7

A Whirlwind Solution

After a hearty breakfast, the two men in the
television van drove off to look for the search-
party, as Minnie Doyle had suggested.

'Follow this lane until you come to a gateway
with a big pile of muck and a milk-churn. Then
start walking across the fields.'

'Wild goose chase?' wondered Orbury after
half a mile of muddy lane.

'Could be, in more ways than one.'

'Suppose we keep on, then, and do a piece on that sinking supermarket instead?'

This new resolve was strengthened when they turned a corner and saw just how big Minnie's pile of muck really was. They were so busy taking it in that they almost missed seeing the obstacle in their path. Jostling suddenly applied his brakes. Two grubby, wild young boys were rushing towards the van, waving frantically. Jostling wound down the window.

'Anything wrong?'

'Plenty!' panted Lenny Hargreaves. 'We've just found a flying saucer full of stamps and postal orders.'

Orbury groaned. 'Oh, not another flying saucer!'

Jostling climbed out of the van. 'Now, take a couple of deep breaths, calm down and start again. At the beginning.'

'You don't believe us, do you?'

'We're not surprised. Nobody ever believes a thing we say.'

'We're always right, as well. But by the time folks decide to take notice it's usually too late.'

'Did I say I didn't believe you? You haven't given me a chance.' Jostling sat down carefully on a bit of grass verge and motioned the boys to join him. Orbury came too.

'Now then, from the beginning.'

'Well, he has this conjuring outfit that a princess once gave him. It had some luminous paint in it, and we got this umbrella. . . .'

'We thought if there was a ghost more people would come, you see. . . .'

'Just a minute! What has all this to do with a flying saucer?'

'You said start at the beginning.'

'I meant start by telling who you are.'

Of course, the minute Jake and Lenny did that, Jostling realised they were the two missing boys from the Ivy Tea Garden. Without waiting to hear any more, he bundled the boys into the van. 'Come on! The sooner we put your auntie out of her misery the better.'

'But we haven't told you about the flying saucer yet.'

'All in good time.' Orbury glanced hopefully at his watch. Maybe they could fit in some early elevenses.

When she saw the boys, Aunt Ivy actually burst into tears, a phenomenon which Jake had never witnessed before. He found it quite gratifying to have been missed so badly, though he guessed that retribution would be on its way when his mum found out. 'Serve us right, too,' he thought, feeling sorry for the upset.

'Two hot baths and two big breakfasts, I should think!' Minnie Doyle was already rummaging in the fridge. Yet, hungry as they were, the boys could not bear the agony of remaining unbelieved.

'Please, Aunt Ivy, just let us show somebody the flying saucer first. We'll be right back.'

Lenny turned to Jostling. 'You could drive us there in five minutes. Would you?'

But by now Aunt Ivy had pulled herself together. Nothing would be allowed to take precedence over baths, clean clothes and at least a hot drink. What was more, Aunt Ivy had no intention of letting the boys out of her sight again just yet. If they went off in the van, then she was coming, too. So in the end, while

Minnie cleaned up the bath, put the boys' clothes to soak, and went to work on gigantic breakfast preparations, the rest of them drove in the van back to the spot where Jostling had picked up the boys.

'It's just down there!' Lenny pointed over a fence to the second field in view. Orbury thought he could just see the top of something silver gleaming in the sunlight. He reached for his camera.

Lenny took the lead, sprinting ahead in his eagerness to prove himself right. He had been anxious in case the saucer had flown, but he need not have worried. There it sat, exactly as before.

As soon as Aunt Ivy caught sight of the 'saucer' she could not help smiling. 'You know what that is? It's the top off the band-stand in Bottlecombe Park.'

'You what?'

'You mean—it blew off in the gale?'

'Then how do you account for these?' Lenny produced the wad of stamps and postal orders, which so far he had managed to keep hidden, having transferred them from one set of 'magic' pockets to another.

Everyone gathered round to look, and Aunt Ivy remembered that, according to Constable Waddle, a man in a stocking-mask had made off with all the stamps and postal orders from Bottlecombe Post Office yesterday morning. Quite a crowd of people had given chase, and the thief had fled across the park, where he finally disappeared among the trees.

'But not before he'd hidden his loot, it seems.'

'And *we* found it!'

'Hey, I'll bet I know where the thief is, as well. He's hiding in the woods. Remember that bobbing glow we saw last night?'

'If he is in there, the search-party will soon flush him out. So in a way, we'll have found *him* as well! Not bad eh, Jake?'

Orbury had been working on his camera, which he now hoisted on to his shoulder. 'Well, I think all this is worth a mention on the news. What say you, Jostling?'

Jostling waved his clip-board at Lenny.

'Back to that hole and peer into it, like you did the first time. That should make a good shot. And you, Jake; what were you doing at the time?'

'Wielding my trusty club. Like this.'

'Ow! Mind the camera! Right then, in a minute I'm going to start asking you some questions. Answer them clearly and slowly, and don't both start talking at once. . . .'

8
Ghost Garden

'We're on the telly!' Jake called to Minnie as they arrived back home. 'You'll be able to see us on tonight's news.'

'Good thing you had them baths, then.' Minnie began serving up a hearty meal.

'Pity the Tea Garden couldn't have been in the film, though,' grumbled Lenny. 'That's just the sort of publicity we were looking for. We seem to have done everything except what we set out to do, which was to put Aunt Ivy on the map.'

Jostling had to agree that it certainly was a lovely garden.

'Couldn't we take another shot or two, then—sort of, showing where the boy heroes live?"

'No,' said Orbury firmly. 'News has to be filmed as and where it happens. You can't go adding bits on for fun. It's got to be as genuine as possible.'

'In that case, Jake and I should still have been dirty and messed up.'

'Tell you what, though, Lenny—you've given me an idea!' Jostling looked suddenly excited, though his eye was on the boys, not the garden. Could they both be destined to end up slurping soup in some commercial? But Jostling would not be drawn. 'Needs pondering yet awhile. We'll let you know if anything comes of it. In fact, if anything does, we'll be back in a few days with a friend of ours.'

'I'll bet they will!' sneered Jake as the van finally drove away. 'They only said that to cheer us up.'

'Well, at least we had one good adventure, and your Aunt Ivy must have made a bit of profit out of all those breakfasts.'

'Not her! Do you know what she did? She fed all the searchers *free* on account of them looking for us.'

'I sometimes wonder if your Aunt Ivy really *wants* to get rich. It could be we're just wasting our time.'

Just then a distant commotion heralded the return of the search-party—with a prisoner. This, they proclaimed, was the Post Office thief, caught sheltering miserably in the woods under a strange-looking silver umbrella.

'Bet he pinched *that*, as well! Though we can't think where from.'

For the moment, Lenny and Jake felt it wiser to say nothing more, especially as Aunt Ivy had just promised to take them to Bottlecombe Fair on Saturday.

'Aren't you mad at us?' Lenny marvelled. He couldn't imagine his mum taking him to the fair after all the upset he'd caused. Life was full

of surprises.

It was certainly a surprise for Jake and Lenny to see themselves on television, for they looked like a couple of strangers.

'That's not really us, is it?' asked Jake, even further bemused by the name-tags which read JACOB ALLEN AND LEONARD HARGREAVES.

'Pity your Aunt Ivy hasn't a video-recorder. We need to get used to it.'

'Think yourself lucky you've seen it at all. She's only had her telly for six months. Before that, she just used to play Patience and crochet these wiggly yellow mats, and listen to "Woman's Hour" on the radio.'

'They've no business to go cutting bits out of the news, though. Especially after what Orbury said about trying to be genuine. You know when Jostling was interviewing me? I said all that about my conjuring, and none of it was in the programme. Not a word!'

'He's probably jealous.'

Friday seemed flat after all the excitement. Even Saturday's fair was a mixed blessing. Jake won a plastic frog for his baby sister, but Lenny lost forty pence on the 'roll-your-own-pennies'. Also, although the bumper cars were fun, the ghost train turned out to be a miserable fiasco. Sunday morning poured with rain, and the boys' mood was one of gloom. Yet had they but known it, Sunday was plump with surprises.

Just before lunch-time the rain stopped, the sun came out and a smart blue car drew up at Ivy's gate. Three men stepped out of it—Jostling, Orbury and their promised friend. The friend was a distinguished gentleman with white hair and expensive clothes, who gazed thoughtfully around him like someone completely new to fields and trees.

Jostling and Orbury waved as they came up the path. 'Told you we'd be back!'

'You only said you might.'

'Anyway, we didn't believe you,' Jake said frankly. 'People never do come back here.'

'They will!' Orbury winked at Jostling.

Aunt Ivy came out to greet her visitors and asked if they would stay to lunch.

'Yes, please. We'll take the table with the best view. We've brought Miles Pellington with us.'

('I hope they're going to pay,' whispered Lenny to Jake.)

It was obvious that Jostling expected the name Miles Pellington to cause a sensation, but however famous that gentleman might be in the television world, Aunt Ivy had clearly never heard of him. She simply fetched a cloth and began wiping up the rain from the best table-top.

'A beautiful spot you live in,' Miles told Ivy. 'Most photogenic bit of countryside I've seen for a long time.'

'I wouldn't live anywhere else.'

'Not even after all this scandal? Perhaps you haven't seen the Sunday papers?' Orbury handed his own copy to Aunt Ivy. 'Your Post Office "thief" had an alibi, after all, it seems. He'd only spent the night in the woods because he'd quarrelled with his wife. I see they've arrested the *Bugle* editor instead.'

'Wow! Let's have a look!' Jake began reading bits of the story out loud, while Lenny and Aunt Ivy listened in astonishment. ' "I meant to return the stamps and postal orders in a day or

276

two," Mr Grubb told the police. "I only did it to make some news. Nothing ever happens in Bottlecombe."'

Orbury grinned mysteriously at Jostling. 'If only he'd waited a bit longer, eh?'

It was roast chicken for lunch, preceded by delicious home-made vegetable soup and followed by perfect strawberry tart and cream. Jake and Lenny watched anxiously from the kitchen window in case the guests should want seconds, or even thirds, of strawberry tart, leaving none for them to have later. But all was well, and when the coffee was ready Miles invited Ivy and the boys to join them at the table.

By now, that Sunday had turned into a perfect summer's day. Even Ivy herself thought she had never seen the countryside looking lovelier. The garden was certainly at its best, all fresh and sparkling after the rain, and Ivy could not help feeling a little glow of pride as she glanced around.

Miles Pellington came straight to the point. 'My dear lady, we have a proposition to put to

you.' He was, it seemed, a programme produ-
cer of the highest standing, and about to
embark upon a series called 'Ghost Garden'.
'Six programmes to start with, but if it proves
popular we can stretch to many more.' The
programme would be separate stories about

different uncanny dramas from the past, which had all happened in or around the same country garden. With unrestrained enthusiasm Miles concluded: 'And yours is the very garden we've been looking for.'

Lenny and Jake sat frog-eyed, and it was

obvious that Aunt Ivy, too, had been taken completely by surprise. Her face changed colours like a scared chameleon, and she darted her anxious gaze from one man to another. 'What—what would I have to do?'

'Why, nothing, except hire us your garden—and keep on providing these wonderful meals for our cast.'

'Plus all the visitors you'll have when the series becomes famous,' Jostling added.

'Hey, that's terrific!' Lenny said at last. 'You'll be really rich, Aunt Ivy.'

'And famous,' added Jake, getting his priorities right.

'Yes—I suppose so,' Aunt Ivy whispered with a touch of regret. She had often wished the garden were more successful, but now, perversely, she could not help thinking of the trampling hordes destroying the peace of her bit of countryside. Then there was all that extra cooking, not to mention the washing-up. She would have to take on help, and help was not always what it should be these days. All the same, one must not be ungrateful. She smiled bravely round the table.

'I expect you've already planned the first six stories?' Lenny enquired. 'If not, I think I could help you. One story could be about this boy magician, who puts on a show in this ghost garden and finds he has really made his friend disappear in a trick called "The Vanishing Accomplice". There's this double fold in the curtain, and the friend's supposed to hide in that, but when he whisks it away . . . .'

Orbury laughed. 'A good try, Lenny, but Miles never works with dogs or children.' Lenny looked hurt.

'Pity. Especially since without me and Jake you'd never have found this place.'

'How do you make that out, Lenny? Don't forget we came here in response to a tip-off from the newspaper. . .'

'. . . telling you Dave Doyle had seen a UFO.'

'. . . which turned out to be a band-stand roof flying through the air.'

'No, that's where you're wrong. Dave had seen our umbrella.' Lenny felt that nobody would ever prove otherwise. 'Anyway, if we hadn't gone after the umbrella we'd never have found the Post Office loot, so you wouldn't have got your story.'

'And Mr Grubb would have sneaked the stuff back and maybe got away with it.'

Orbury admitted the truth of this, and pointed out that the stunning shots he had taken of the 'saucer' and surrounding countryside were the shots which had really caught Miles's interest.

'You see?' crowed Jake. 'In any case, Lenny was the one who thought of a ghost garden in the first place. The Haunted Ivy Tea Garden. He'd been planning it since last Wednesday.'

'And I've been planning it for a year and a half,' grinned Miles. 'Ask Jocelyn and Aubrey if you don't believe me.'

Lenny Hargreaves smiled a superior smile. 'I believe you,' he said generously. 'Great minds think alike.'

Other great reads from **Red Fox**

Further Red Fox titles that you might enjoy reading are listed on the following pages. They are available in bookshops or they can be ordered directly from us.

If you would like to order books, please send this form and the money due to:

ARROW BOOKS, BOOKSERVICE BY POST, PO BOX 29, DOUGLAS, ISLE OF MAN, BRITISH ISLES. Please enclose a cheque or postal order made out to Arrow Books Ltd for the amount due, plus 22p per book for postage and packing, both for orders within the UK and for overseas orders.

NAME _____

ADDRESS _____

_____

Please print clearly.

Whilst every effort is made to keep prices low, it is sometimes necessary to increase cover prices at short notice. If you are ordering books by post, to save delay it is advisable to phone to confirm the correct price. The number to ring is THE SALES DEPARTMENT 071 (if outside London) 973 9700.

Other great reads ⟵ *from* **Red Fox**

THE SNIFF STORIES   Ian Whybrow

Things just keep happening to Ben Moore. It's dead hard
avoiding disaster when you've got to keep your street cred with
your mates *and* cope with a family of oddballs at the same time.
There's his appalling 2½ year old sister, his scatty parents who
are into healthy eating and animal rights and, worse than all
of these, there's Sniff! If only Ben could just get on with his
scientific experiments and his attempt at a world beating
Swampbeast score . . . but there's no chance of that while chaos
is just around the corner.

ISBN 0 09 9750406   £2.50

J.B. SUPERSLEUTH   Joan Davenport

James Bond is a small thirteen-year-old with spots and
spectacles. But with a name like that, how can he help being
a supersleuth?

It all started when James and 'Polly' (Paul) Perkins spotted
a teacher's stolen car. After that, more and more mysteries
needed solving. With the case of the Arabian prince, the
Murdered Model, the Bonfire Night Murder and the Lost
Umbrella, JB's reputation at Moorside Comprehensive soars.

But some of the cases aren't quite what they seem . . .

ISBN 0 09 9717808   £1.99

Other great reads ✆ *from* **Red Fox**

Discover the exciting and hilarious books of Hazel Townson!

THE MOVING STATUE

One windy day in the middle of his paper round, Jason Riddle is blown against the town's war memorial statue.

But the statue moves its foot! Can this be true?

ISBN 0 09 973370 6   £1.99

ONE GREEN BOTTLE

Tim Evans has invented a fantasic new board game called REDUNDO. But after he leaves it at his local toy shop it disappears! Could Mr Snyder, the wily toy shop owner have stolen the game to develop it for himself? Tim and his friend Doggo decide to take drastic action and with the help of a mysterious green bottle, plan a Reign of Terror.

ISBN 0 09 956810 1   £1.50

THE SPECKLED PANIC

When Kip buys Venger's Speckled Truthpaste instead of toothpaste, funny things start happening. But they get out of control when the headmaster eats some by mistake. What terrible truths will he tell the parents on speech day?

ISBN 0 09 935490 X   £1.75

THE CHOKING PERIL

In this sequel to *The Speckled Panic*, Herbie, Kip and Arthur Venger the inventor attempt to reform Grumpton's litterbugs.

ISBN 0 09 950530 4   £1.25

Other great reads ❦ *from* **Red Fox**

Discover the great animal stories of Colin Dann

JUST NUFFIN

The Summer holidays loomed ahead with nothing to look forward to except one dreary week in a caravan with only Mum and Dad for company. Roger was sure he'd be bored.

But then Dad finds Nuffin: an abandoned puppy who's more a bundle of skin and bones than a dog. Roger's holiday is transformed and he and Nuffin are inseparable. But Dad is adamant that Nuffin must find a new home. Is there *any* way Roger can persuade him to change his mind?

ISBN 0 09 966900 5   £1.99

KING OF THE VAGABONDS

'You're very young,' Sammy's mother said, 'so heed my advice. Don't go into Quartermile Field.'

His mother and sister are happily domesticated but Sammy, the tabby cat, feels different. They are content with their lot, never wondering what lies beyond their immediate surroundings. But Sammy is burningly curious and his life seems full of mysteries. Who is his father? Where has he gone? And what is the mystery of Quartermile Field?

ISBN 0 09 957190 0   £2.50

Other great reads **from** *Red Fox*

Discover the wide range of exciting activity books from Red Fox

THE PAINT AND PRINT FUN BOOK
Steve and Megumi Biddle

Would you like to make a glittering bird? A colourful tiger? A stained-glass window? Or an old treasure map? Well, all you need are ordinary materials like vegetables, tinfoil, paper doilies, even your own fingers to make all kinds of amazing things—without too much mess.

Follow Steve and Megumi's step-by-step instructions and clear diagrams and you can make all kinds of professional designs—to hang on your wall or give to your friends.

ISBN 0 09 9644606 £2.50

CRAZY KITES   Peter Eldin

This book is a terrific introduction to the art of flying kites. There are lots of easy-to-assemble, different kites to make, from the basic flat kite to the Chinese dragon and the book also gives you clear instructions on launching, flying and landing. Kite flying is fun. Help yourself to a soaring good time.

ISBN 0 09 964550 5   £2.50

Other great reads from **Red Fox**

AMAZING ORIGAMI FOR CHILDREN
Steve and Megumi Biddle

Origami is an exciting and easy way to make toys, decorations and all kinds of useful things from folded paper.

Use leftover gift paper to make a party hat and a fancy box. Or create a colourful lorry, a pretty rose and a zoo full of origami animals. There are over 50 fun projects in Amazing Origami.

Following Steve and Megumi's step-by-step instructions and clear drawings, you'll amaze your friends and family with your magical paper creations.

ISBN 0 09 9661802   £4.99

MAGICAL STRING   Steve and Megumi Biddle

With only a loop of string you can make all kinds of shapes, puzzles and games. Steve and Megumi Biddle provide all the instructions and diagrams that are needed to create their amazing string magic in another of their inventive and absorbing books.

ISBN 0 09 964470 3   £2.50